The Corn Raid

James Lincoln Collier

JAMESTOWN PUBLISHERS

a division of NTC/CONTEMPORARY PUBLISHING GROUP
Lincolnwood, Illinois USA

Cover Credits
  Design: Herman Adler Design Group
  Illustration: David Schweitzer
  Timeline: North Wind

ISBN: 0-8092-0578-5 (hardbound)
ISBN: 0-8092-0619-6 (softbound)

Published by Jamestown Publishers,
a division of NTC/Contemporary Publishing Group, Inc.,
4255 West Touhy Avenue,
Lincolnwood (Chicago), Illinois 60646-1975 U.S.A.

90 ML 0 9 8 7 6 5 4 3 2 1

Chapter 1

I was kneeling in the dirt, weeding around the tobacco seedlings. It was only April, but by 10 o'clock in the morning the sun was already hot on my back and the earth had that dry smell that it gets. It would have been easier to grub out the weeds with the hoe, but if I got careless with the hoe I could knock over one of the seedlings, and Laydon would whip me for it good. Laydon liked whipping his servants. To be safe I'd put the hoe down and was weeding the seedlings by hand.

Someday I'd be big and would get away from Laydon. I was 12 and pretty strong for my age because of all those years of hard work I'd done, but I wasn't big enough yet. If I ran off he'd catch me easy, and the governor would make me go back to him. But someday when I was bigger, I would. It was all I ever thought about. Day and night I planned out how I was going to do it and what I was going to do when I was free. It gave me hope.

I was going along like that, thinking about not being a servant anymore, when I saw something move at the edge of the woods that grew along the bottom of the tobacco field. I stood up and looked over there, shielding my eyes with my hand. Beyond the line of trees was the James River. Nothing moved. There was no breeze. It might have been an animal that I saw. There was no shortage of squirrels and possums in those woods. Deer too. They could move mighty quick through the woods and disappear on you in a second.

I knelt down again. My knees had hardly hit the dirt when I saw another flash of movement. I looked up. An Indian boy was running off through the trees. I remembered that I had left the hoe over there somewhere. A shock went through me. I jumped up and began shouting, "Mr. Laydon, Mr. Laydon!" Then I was running after the Indian boy as fast as I could go across the field of tobacco seedlings. A hoe was a valuable thing in Virginia. If that Indian boy got away with ours, Laydon would blow up like gunpowder and whip me until I could hardly walk.

The Indian had got a good start on me. He was used to slipping and sliding through the woods. I was going to have a mighty hard time catching up with him, and I got that bad feeling where you're desperate for something to come out right but you know it isn't going to. Maybe I'd have some luck. Maybe he'd trip and twist his ankle on a root or something. I raced across the fields and into the woods. I could see the Indian ahead of me, going for the river, just a flash here and there as he slipped around the trees. "Hey!" I shouted. "Drop that hoe." Then I shouted, "Mr. Laydon, there's an Indian stole the hoe!" The Indians loved our hoes. They loved our axes, shovels, knives, swords—anything made of metal. They didn't have any metal, only stone and wood tools, which were pretty

2

good for what they were but not up to metal ones. Why had I been so careless? Why hadn't I kept that blame hoe close to me? What the devil was I thinking about? I tried to come up with some excuse, like the hoe was laying right next to me and the Indian crept up behind me and grabbed it. Something. Anything. Laydon would say he'd learn me about being careless with other people's property, and he'd whip me until my tail was swelled up and puffy when you touched it, and I wouldn't be able to sit down for a week. Oh, I hated him when he whipped me. It didn't happen more than two or three times a year, but the awfulness of it stuck for a long time.

I hit the woods. The Indian boy had turned and was running along the edge of the James River, where the trees came down to the bank. Suddenly I realized that he'd cornered himself. Ahead of him was a place where a creek ran down into the river. It was marshy there, a big patch of reeds. You couldn't swim through it and it was hard to walk through, for the bottom was all mushy. If he went into the marsh, I'd be able to catch up with him easy.

Then what would I do? Did he have a knife or a hatchet? I felt in my belt for my knife to make sure it hadn't fallen out of its scabbard while I was running. What was I going to do, attack him with my knife? Suppose he had a knife. Would we have a knife fight? I sure hoped not. I'd never done anything like that. Fought a lot back in London when I was six and in the street gang, but that was with hands and feet, not knives. Maybe when he saw that he was cornered he'd drop the hoe and run off through the marsh.

I wondered–did he have a canoe tied up somewhere? I didn't believe so. It was mighty hard work for the Indians to carve a canoe out of a big log; they wouldn't let a boy go off in one alone just to steal a hoe. He'd be coming to the marshy place where the creek came into the river soon. "Mr. Laydon, help!" I shouted, mostly to give the Indian the idea that a man was coming along behind me.

Then through the trees ahead of me I saw the Indian standing still, his back to me, looking into the marsh. There was a little clearing there, where the creek met the river. He heard my footsteps thumping on the ground and swirled around to face me. I came out of the woods into the clearing and stopped, still trying to figure out a way to get that hoe away from him without a knife fight.

We were about 20 feet apart. He wasn't wearing anything but a loincloth—belt around his waist and a piece of leather going through his legs. I didn't see a knife anywhere on him; I was mighty glad of that. But he had the hoe. I was feeling mighty worried. How was I going to get close enough to him to stick a knife into him? I'd never stuck a knife into anybody. I hated the idea of it. But if he didn't give up the hoe, I'd have to do it—try to, anyway. I took a deep breath. "Drop the hoe," I said, as firm as I could.

"You can't make me," he said.

"Oh, yes I can." I took out my knife. "You don't belong on our land anyway." Saying that made me feel kind of uneasy. It'd been Indian land first. But we had paid them something for it. Leastwise, I reckoned we had.

Whatever the rights of it, it was our land now.

He didn't say anything, but he raised up the hoe, ready to swing at me. We were both sweating. His skin was tannish. The right half of his head was shaved clean. The Indians did that so their hair wouldn't get tangled in their bowstrings when they drew their bows. On the left side of his head, his hair was long and woven into a braid. A drop of sweat rolled down his chest, across his belly, and into his belt. His belly moved up and down as he breathed. It gave me a funny feeling to se his belly move like that. He was the same as me—probably good and scared and wondering how to get out of this. I reckoned he figured he was the one who was in a fix, not me. He stole a hoe and got caught at it, and now he was in a trap. It made me feel a little more confident to realize that he must figure I had the upper hand. "Look," I said, "My master's bound to be here in a minute with his musket. He'll shoot you dead like as not. Drop the hoe, run off through the marsh, and I won't chase you."

"No," he said. "You go away or I kill you."

He wasn't going to give in without a fight. I could see that. I'd have to fight him. I took another deep breath. "I'm warning you. When my master comes, he'll shoot you dead. Or take you over to the fort and they'll hang you. Which would you like better?"

He waggled the hoe at me. "You don't scare me with big talk."

I don't know which I hated worse—the idea of getting whacked in the head with the hoe or having to stick a knife into him. Not that killing was a new thing out in Virginia. We'd killed plenty of Indians and they'd killed plenty of us English.

Sooner or later he was going to charge. That was the Indian way. I looked at his bare sweaty flesh, trying to figure out where to shove the knife. Should I try to push it through his chest into his heart, which would kill him on the spot? Or should I stick it into his belly, where it was soft but wouldn't kill him right off? I was all shaky inside. I swallowed and took another deep breath.

He charged, the hoe cocked back over his shoulder, both hands down at the end of the handle. He was expecting to get a good swing at my head before I could duck. I saw in a flash that if I charged too, maybe I could get in close before he could swing the hoe. I charged.

It took him by surprise. He started to swing, but by the time he got the hoe uncocked and coming around at me, I was too close for him to get in a good hit. I raised my hand to ward off the hoe handle. It caught me on the back of the wrist and hurt like blazes. I shoved the knife at him. He tried to twist away from it, but he was still coming toward me fast and he lost his balance. He got out of the way of the knife, and we slammed into each other. But he was already off balance, and down he went. He flipped over onto his back and raised his feet toward me, but I skittered around his legs and bent my knees, ready to drop on him knife first.

And then Laydon shouted, "Stop for the Lord's sake, Richard!"

I swung around and the Indian boy sat up. Laydon

was standing at the edge of the clearing, his musket leveled at the Indian boy. I looked at the Indian. He sat there frozen, his face dead still. My heart was just pounding, and now that it was all over I was all atremble. It was the first time in the whole six years I been Laydon's servant that I was glad to see him.

Was he going to kill the Indian boy? Nobody would have said anything if he'd done it. He'd caught the Indian stealing. One Indian boy more or less didn't count for anything, anyway. Suddenly I felt sorry for the boy. He didn't move a muscle. He sat there with nothing on his face, waiting to be shot. I figured that must be a mighty awful feeling. I was glad it wasn't me who was sitting there staring at that hole in the musket barrel.

Laydon lowered the musket and came into the clearing. "What's this all about, Richard?"

"I caught him stealing the hoe, sir."

"How come it was laying where he could get a hold of it?" He was looking for a chance to give somebody a whipping out of it.

"Honest, sir, I wasn't more than five feet from it. I was working over near the edge of the woods. He slipped up through the trees when I was facing the other way, snatched it, and ran." It was a pack of lies, of course. I'd been out in the middle of the field when it happened.

"You must have been snoozing."

"Honest, sir, I wasn't snoozing. If I'd been snoozing I wouldn't notice him at all, and he would've got clean away."

He frowned, for he hadn't found an excuse to whip

me. After all, I'd chased the Indian out here and might have got myself killed for it.

He turned to the Indian boy. "You speak English?"

"I speak English good." Some of them did. The Indians and the English had been trading with each other when they weren't fighting or having peace conferences the whole 12 years since the first settlers came in 1607. Some Indians would work for English to earn a musket or an ax, although they never stayed at it long. And until the new governor came in and put in stricter rules, the Indians would come into Jamestown for one thing or another. Some of them had picked up a lot of English.

"What tribe are you from?" Laydon said.

"Weyanocks."

"One of the Powhatans? Opechancanough's people?"

"Yes," he said. Most of the Indians in our part of Virginia had been under one great chief, Powhatan. His daughter was named Pocahontas. She had married John Rolfe, the Englishman who figured out how to grow good tobacco here in Virginia. Powhatan had been sort of friendly to us, but he died awhile back and his brother Opechancanough had taken over. Things between us and the Indians weren't so easy now.

Laydon poked the musket barrel towards the Indian to remind him of it. "What's your name?"

"Weetoppin." I had to admire him. As far as he knew, there was still a good chance he would be shot or taken over to Jamestown to be hanged. Yet his face was just as calm and still as ice on a pond. I wondered what it would be like to have him for a friend. I didn't have many

8

friends—didn't have any my own age, when you got down to it. They sent English boys here sometimes to be indentured servants like me, but most of them died of sickness before they got seasoned. I was lucky and stayed alive until I was seasoned—got good and sick that first winter, but I didn't die. Once you got seasoned, you were likely to live for a while.

Laydon poked the gun barrel toward the Indian again. "All right, Weetoppin, on your feet. Let's go."

"What are you going to do with him, sir?" I asked.

"Take him home for now. Maybe we'll keep him."

Chapter 2

Some of the Virginia settlers had lots of indentured servants—seven or eight maybe. A lot of settlers didn't have any. Mr. Laydon had two, me and Susan Cooper. Laydon bought Susan's indenture when she came over in 1614, when Mr. Rolfe sold his first lot of tobacco and everyone realized how much money was to be made in it, if you had the hands to work the fields. Most indentures were for seven years, so Susan had only two more years to go and she'd be free of Laydon. He got me for nothing, and worth every penny of it he always said. Back in London nobody wanted me, so they shipped me over to Virginia. But nobody wanted me in Virginia either. A six-year-old couldn't do enough work to pay for his feed and would probably die before he got big enough to be of any use. But somebody had to take me, so the governor had some people draw lots. Laydon lost and got stuck with me. At first, being a little kid and not knowing much about anything, I was happy. I never had a family before, never lived in a real house that I could remember, and here I was going into what looked like a family to me. But I learned better real soon. Laydon liked the sound of it when he whacked me on the tail, liked to see if he could get a real scream out of me. Once I figured that out, though, I got determined not to scream and would clench my mouth tight. That would just get him madder, and he'd go at me with a flat board that he'd hung on a string by the fireplace where it'd be handy when he needed it. Once after he'd beaten me, Susan said, "Richard, don't be silly. Let out a good yelp the first time he whacks you and get it over with."

"Never," I said, the tears running down my cheeks. "I don't care if he kills me."

"He might someday if he loses hold of himself."

"I don't care," I said, rubbing my eyes.

The fact was, for the first couple of years, Laydon was waiting for me to die. He had set me to work weeding tobacco but it didn't pay for my keep, according to him. My food and clothes cost money. So did carting me over to Jamestown every Sunday for church, for the governor insisted that all children were to be churched and raised as good Christians. I took his word for it that I was a terrible burden and expense, for I was little and didn't know what things cost. But when I got older and had some sense about it, I could see well enough that a chunk of cornbread and some roast pork wasn't any great expense, and a couple of shirts and a pair of trousers were even less. I hadn't had shoes on my feet since the bottoms wore off the ones I wore over from London.

Laydon expected me to die, so when I got that terrible sickness during my first winter in Virginia, he told Susan not to waste food on me. Of course, she fixed me broth and such things and kept me fed up, and by and by, I got better.

By the time I was eight, Laydon had changed his tune. I was big enough to be a real help. That was when he started explaining to me that I hadn't been indentured in the regular fashion, with the terms written out on a piece of paper. He said that I couldn't expect to be out of indenture until I was a grown man. When I asked him how old I had to be for that, he'd only say, "I'll let you know when the time comes." But I knew better than to trust his word.

Anyway, I understood why he wanted the Indian boy. Laydon had enough land to grow a fair amount of tobacco on, but the land wasn't any use without hands to work it. Before I came over he'd had three servants, but two of them died, leaving only Susan. He was trying to build up some money to buy more servants, but in the meantime he had to make do with me and Susan. If he could get the Indian boy to work for him, it would help a good deal.

We walked the Indian boy back along the James River—him first, then Laydon with the musket, and then me carrying the hoe. Would the Indian really agree to live with us? When you got down to it, there was no way you could keep an Indian if he didn't want to stay with you. He'd run off when your back was turned and disappear into the woods. English servants didn't have the same chance. They had no place to run except to go live with the Indians, which most of them didn't want to do. On top of it, sometimes the governor executed people who ran off to the Indians if he caught them—broke a couple of them on the wheel. Running off was risky.

I hoped Laydon could make a deal with the Indian boy. I was just desperate to have a friend. I was tired of working all by myself in the tobacco fields from sunup to sundown. It would be wonderful to have somebody to talk to.

I wondered what the Indian boy was thinking— Weepin, or whatever he said his name was. Did he still think we were going to kill him? I peered around Laydon to get a look at him. All I could see was his back, stiff and straight, as he walked along. Was he trying to make himself brave so he would die like a man? What would I have done in his place? Would I take it like a man if the Indians were torturing me the way they tortured prisoners—breaking my bones one at a time or holding my feet in the fire, first one foot, then the other, then a hand, and so forth? The Indians did that to each other when they took prisoners, and they did it a couple times to the English too. Would I keep my mouth shut and not blink my eyes? Or would I start crying and begging them to stop?

We came out into the tobacco field and crossed to the house. There wasn't much to the house. I'd helped Mr. Laydon build it right after I came from England. We'd lived in the fort—Jamestown—while we were building it. Laydon did most of the work, I admit. He carved beams out of tree trunks with an adze and then put together a frame. Then he filled in the frame to make walls with saplings woven into kind of a mat. Next, he smeared the mat with a mix of mud, clay, and straw. That's what I helped with, mixing up the mud and clay in a bucket, while he plastered it on. The stuff was almost hard as rock when it set up. The roof was thatch—bundles of straw set just so. The house was tight enough, but small.

Susan was standing in the doorway, watching us cross the field. Her hair was yellow and shining in the sun. I always liked looking at her. "Why, he's just a boy," she said as we came up to her.

"It's a good thing I got there when I did," Laydon said. "Richard and the Indian were about to kill each other." No credit to me.

"Richard, what possessed you?" Susan said. "You might have got yourself killed."

I reckoned I was entitled to some credit out of it. I'd been brave enough, it seemed to me, even though I had been mighty scared. "I chased him down to where the creek comes into the marsh and trapped him there. He came at me with the hoe, but I was too quick for him and tripped him up. I was about to take his scalp when Mr. Laydon came along and saved him." It wasn't too much of a lie, only a little one.

"If the blame boy hadn't left the hoe laying where the Indian could get it, he wouldn't have got himself into trouble like that."

"Richard, you shouldn't have taken the chance," Susan said, "risking your life for a hoe."

"It was right next to me," I said, beginning to get angry. That was a lie but I didn't care, for nobody was willing to give me any credit. "What was I supposed to do, let him run off with it?"

"Richard, watch your tongue," Laydon said. "Susan, fix us our dinner."

We got out of the hot sun and into the coolness of the house. I always liked going into that coolness on a hot day. It had a happy feeling to it. Susan already had dinner on the table. Roast pork and cornbread. It was too early in the year for berries or beans or vegetables like squash. I got mighty tired of pork and cornbread by the end of spring, but it beat going hungry—which I'd done in the spring sometimes when I was little.

Food was always a problem in the early days of Jamestown. First couple of years most of them starved to death, or died from sickness because they were weak from want of food. Things got better more recent, especially since Rolfe figured out a way to grow good tobacco in Virginia. That Indian tobacco around there couldn't compare with the tobacco they were growing in the Caribbean. But Rolfe, he got a type going that was pretty good, and finally the money started to roll in. But back then, I went to bed pretty often with nothing in my belly but a piece of cornbread.

Susan nodded at the Indian. "He eating with us, sir?"

"Set a place for him." Then he looked at the Indian. "You could eat something, couldn't you, Weetoppin?"

We all looked at him. I never saw an Indian who couldn't eat. It was their way—eat everything in sight when they had the chance, then go hungry without complaining when hard times came.

The Indian boy stood there looking at that food—the wooden platter full of squares of cornbread hot and smoking, another platter full of roast pork smelling fragrant and spicy, and a pitcher of gravy to pour over everything. He licked his lips. But he was mad at us and didn't want to take anything from us. He turned his head and looked out the window into the tobacco field, where he'd snatched up the hoe an hour ago. I figured he'd give in. Indians were usually pretty hungry in the spring when the corn had run out and the berries and such hadn't come in yet.

He looked back at the table full of food. Suddenly he sat down on the bench at the table. He snatched up a piece of pork with one hand and a piece of cornbread with the other and began ramming them both into his mouth at once.

Laydon laughed. "Go to it, Weetoppin. We've got plenty." Laydon had begun to put away a little money from tobacco. He'd invested in some cows and chickens, which would soon enough produce a calf and more chickens, so we ate pretty good. We all sat and began to eat, and it was quiet in the house except for the sound of spoons scraping on wooden trenchers and a slurp here and there. Weetoppin kept looking around the house as he chewed, observing the things that we had that Indians didn't have—the fireplace poker, the great ladle hanging by the fireplace, the iron stew-pot, the pewter mug that Laydon had inherited from his grandfather who'd had a nice farm up in Derbyshire, north of London. I could see in Weetoppin's eyes that he was curious about all these things.

When we were done eating, Susan picked up the dishes and took them outside to wash them in the bucket. Laydon looked Weetoppin up and down. "Well," he said, "you were mighty hungry, weren't you, Weetoppin?"

"Starving time for Weyanocks. We don't eat nothing but fish for long time. English got our corn."

"That's the Weyanocks' fault. You traded corn for things. I remember the deal. Traded for cloth, knives." He paused. "Hoes to make life easier for the women."

"Things better before English come." Weetoppin glared out the window, as though he was seeing the time when the tobacco field was a forest of cedars, hickories, and oaks.

Laydon laughed. "Weetoppin, you don't remember before the English came. How old are you? Twelve? You're too young to remember."

Weetoppin scowled. "Old people told me."

"It's not true that the Indians were better off before," Laydon said. "Look what you got from us. Metal tools, cloth, guns. If only you'd farm like we do, you'd never have starving times. If you Indians had any sense, you'd take up our ways. Nice snug English houses, apple orchards, vegetable gardens, spinning wheels. We never had starving times in England."

"Sir, I went hungry a good deal in London." I said.

He frowned. "That was because we had too many people. The population grew too fast. Nobody would have thought of coming to Virginia if it hadn't been for the population growing so fast. Wouldn't have been any need for it. Why do you think I came? According to the law, my older brother got my pa's farm and there was nothing for me. He said he was sorry for me and would give me my passage to Virginia if I'd go."

"Oh," I said. It didn't surprise me any that somebody wanted to get rid of Laydon, but I didn't say so.

"English so rich," Weetoppin said, "how come they always need corn from Indians?"

Laydon shrugged. "Some of these fellows figure that with the best tobacco three shillings a pound, they can't waste land for corn. They'll take the chance on getting hold of some."

"Steal it from Weyanocks," scowled Weetoppin.

"*Trade* for it. Well, let's forget that. There's plenty of land here for everybody. Let's not argue about it." He leaned back on the bench to rest his shoulders against the wall. "How'd you like to eat like this all the time? We have plenty of corn now, a cow, some chickens. I'm planning on getting a breeding sow too. We don't have starving times like we used to. Indians do. Not us."

It was true that a lot of settlers didn't want to waste time on corn. The governor and the Virginia Company—the English company that founded Jamestown—kept ordering the men to plant corn enough to eat, but all that the settlers wanted to plant was tobacco. They filled every square inch of land with it. They even planted tobacco in the streets of Jamestown. When they needed corn, they'd go out to some Indian village with guns and demand corn. But the Indians might not have it. They might have run out of it themselves or might have hidden it away in the woods somewhere. So we'd go hungry. We'd catch fish if we could, or maybe get lucky and shoot a deer—or if it came to the worst, catch crabs, which were an awful lot of work for the food you got out of them. We went hungry a lot in those days. I tell you, it was no fun. My stomach would burble, and all I'd ever think of was food. See a brown hat and it'd turn into a plum pudding. Hear a crow caw and see a fat bird steaming on a platter. I'd have eaten a crow sometimes too. But the money was rolling in from tobacco now, and people had hogs, cows, hens. We still needed corn from the Indians sometimes, though. But we hadn't had a starving time in about two years.

Laydon looked at Weetoppin. "Well, what about it?"

I wished he would say yes. That was curious, for we'd just had an awful fight where one of us might have got killed. But now that I could see inside him a little—saw him gobble down his food, saw him get curious about our things and all—I realized he wasn't much different from me. Susan worked in the field with me most days for at least part of the time. And of course, Laydon was out there a good deal. But mostly I was out there alone. I could sure use Weetoppin's company.

Weetoppin looked at Laydon. "You teach me shoot a gun?"

"Sure," Laydon said.

Weetoppin licked his lips. "What I going to do?"

"Work," Laydon said, " Just like we do. Same work as us. There's nothing to it. Easiest thing going." That was a lie, but I didn't say so.

"English people work too hard."

"You don't get anywhere if you don't work hard."

Weetoppin considered. "Indians ain't trying to get nowhere. We was all right before the English come."

"That's all right for an Indian. It isn't enough for me. I aim to be rich one of these days. Build myself a big house like Henry Spofford's, with glass in the windows." Henry Spofford was our neighbor up the road. He had lots of land, 8 or 10 servants to work the fields and take care of the house, and he had a horse. A lot of gentlemen like Henry Spofford came out to Virginia to make their fortunes in tobacco. Weren't doing so well back in England, maybe, so they sold their land, indentured some servants, and came over and started growing tobacco. If you got yourselves set up that way it was hard not to make money. We could sell in Europe all the tobacco we could grow.

Suddenly Weetoppin understood that Laydon needed him. He could bargain hard. "What you pay me if I work?" The Indians were good bargainers.

Laydon leaned forward, his hands flat on the table. "Plenty to eat. A warm place to sleep in the winter."

"Weyanocks' house plenty warm."

"A good metal knife," Laydon said.

"Gun too," Weetoppin said.

Laydon shook his head. English weren't supposed to

give Indians guns, although lots of them did. "No gun. I only have one."

Weetoppin thought about it. "Two knives, ax, blanket, shirt."

Laydon laughed. "You're a tough bargainer, Weyanock. Make it a knife and a blanket, and I'll throw in a shirt and pants so you look decent in church."

So Weetoppin came to live with us.

Chapter 3

The curious thing about Weetoppin was that he worked out his whole thing by himself. He didn't bring his father and mother in on it at all. Never mentioned them. I wondered—was he like me and didn't have any father and mother? Or did they maybe send him to indenture himself, so as to get knives and things? It wasn't like the Indians to do that. The Company was all in favor of having Indian children come and live with us. They figured the answer to the Indian problem was to make them English—have them start farms like ours, build houses like ours, go to our church. Then once the Indians became English, there wouldn't be any trouble between us. The best way to make them English was to raise their kids amongst us. They'd be bound to come out English.

But generally speaking, the Indians didn't go along with it. They wanted to stick to their own ways and didn't want their children to become servants of the English. For one thing, the Indians weren't as quick to whip children as some of the English were—Laydon, for one. So it wasn't like an Indian father and mother to let a boy go off to live with the English. Maybe Weetoppin was like me and didn't have anyone to take an interest in him. I resolved to bring it up with him, for it would be a good thing to talk about between us, not having anyone to take an interest in you. Whatever did happen to my father and mother anyway? Did they die? Or did they just decide they didn't want me and threw me away? It made me feel mighty low when I thought about it. Made me feel like I wasn't as good as everybody else—wasn't worth very much. I figured it would help to know somebody else who'd got thrown away. We could talk about it.

But I decided I'd better go easy at first. As it turned out I didn't have much choice about it, for when Laydon sent us out into the field to get on with the weeding, Weetoppin was about as friendly as a snake. I showed him what we had to do, hoping to start a conversation out of it, but all he did was grunt, get down on his knees, and set to work, ignoring me like I wasn't there. Was he sorry to be leaving home? Maybe his father and mother had sent him away and he wished he was back in his village. I tried to think of some conversation that might cheer him up. "Weetoppin, if Laydon goes over to Jamestown this afternoon we might be able to sneak down to the river and go for a swim to cool off. What about that?"

He didn't turn his head, just went on weeding.

"I'm not supposed to do it," I said. "Laydon would smack me around good if he caught me. But I do it anyway. Susan won't say anything."

Weetoppin still didn't look around, just went on weeding.

I was beginning to get exasperated. "Do you know how to swim? I didn't know how when I came over from England, but I taught myself when nobody was looking."

This time he gave me a look, which was an improvement, although it was more of a sneer than a look. Then he went back to his weeding.

"That wasn't such a dumb question. How would I know if you can swim or not?"

Without turning around he said, "I can swim."

"Well, all right then. Do you want to sneak off for a swim?"

He still didn't look up. "Maybe."

Blame him. Why should I go to all the trouble of being nice if he was going to act this way? Still, I wanted to make friends with him. I said, "I guess most Indians around here can swim because there's so much water. Rivers, creeks, the bay, the ocean. I guess you must have learned to swim when you were little. But farther west, where the hills begin, there aren't a lot of rivers deep enough for swimming—maybe those Indians out there can't swim."

"All Indians can swim."

I figured that was a lie. How did he know that all Indians could swim? Did he know all the Indians there were? But I wanted to keep out of an argument with him. "What's out there beyond the fall line? You ever been out there?" The fall line was where the hills started to go up and the river turned into rapids, or waterfalls. All the land west of the fall line was a mystery to us English. We didn't go out there. Too dangerous. I always wondered if there was something real exciting out there. Gold mines, maybe, like the Spanish found down there in Peru. Or maybe strange beasts, like elephants or giant birds with wings as big as a house. I'd never seen an elephant, but I'd heard about them. It would be great if there were things like gold mines and elephants out there beyond the fall line. I hoped that someday I'd be able to go out there myself and see.

"Powhatans don't go out there," Weetoppin said. "Monacans there."

He still wasn't being too agreeable, but maybe I could get a conversation out of it. "Are the Powhatans scared of the Monacans?"

Right away I wished I'd put it different, for he jumped up. "I not going to do this weeding. This women's work." He stalked off to the tree line at the edge of the field and sat down in the shade, his arms folded over his chest.

So that was why he was sore. One reason, anyway. He was right about it. With the Indians, the women and children took care of the gardens and the men did the hunting and fishing. It seemed to the English that the men were mighty lazy, for often enough they'd be lying around in the sun or playing games while the women were sweating over their corn, pumpkins, and beans. The Indian men said they had to save their energy for hunting and fishing. But mostly, it was because gardening was too lowly for them. It wasn't exciting enough.

I went over to Weetoppin. I was getting tired of him sulking all the time. "Look, Weetoppin, if you don't want to do farm work, why'd you agree to it in the first place?"

He looked up at me. "Gardens are for women," he said. "Not for men."

"If Laydon sees you sitting under a tree instead of working, he's liable to give you a whipping."

"Ain't gonna whip me."

"Yes, he will. That's the rule. A master can whip a servant anytime he's got a good excuse. If you're going to live with us, you got to go by our rules."

"English rules no good."

He was mighty exasperating, all right. I was ready to give up on him. I looked up toward the house. You never could tell when Laydon might show up. Sometimes I'd be out in the middle of the tobacco field, hoeing or picking bugs off the plants, with a clear view for a hundred yards in every direction, and he'd pop up out of nowhere. It was like he came out of the ground. It was the strangest thing. "Listen, Weetoppin, Laydon's likely to show up any minute. If you want a whipping, that's all right by me, but I don't want one. I've had too many blame whippings and know what they feel like."

"Nobody whip me, Richard," he said.

It startled me that he used my name. It was a good sign. Still, I didn't want Laydon to catch me standing around, so I left Weetoppin sitting in the shade and went back to work.

About two minutes later Weetoppin was standing over me, looking down at where I was kneeling in the dirt. He'd popped out of the ground just like Laydon. "What he whip you for?"

I sat back on my heels to look up at him. "Anything. Nothing. Sometimes just because he's sore and wants to whip somebody. Maybe the price of tobacco is off a little. Maybe the governor passed some order he didn't like. He'll want to whip somebody for it. You can tell when it's coming: his nose gets fat. Me and Susan, when we see that fat nose, we try to keep out of sight."

"Why don't you kill him?"

"I don't want to get hung. I saw some boys hung back in London once. It made me sick to see their legs jerking around as they were hanging there."

"He don't whip me."

"Well, he will if he wants to," I said. "Weetoppin, if you aren't going to weed, at least kneel down so it looks like you're doing something. He's bound to come out and check up on us pretty soon."

"He don't whip me," he said again. But all the same he knelt down. "What it feel like to get whipped?"

"Mighty bad. It stings like old Ned. I can take that, for it goes away in a couple of days if he doesn't lay into you too hard. The worst thing is him having that power over you. I hate it. I hate it that he can whip me and there's nothing I can do about it. It takes all the insides out of you. Worse than not having anyone to take an interest in you."

I gave him a quick look to see if he'd say something about that, but he didn't. He said, "Next time, you kill him."

"I told you, I don't want to get hung."

Weetoppin shook his head. "Indians don't whip children. My father never whip me."

27

So he had a father at least. I felt disappointed. It wasn't right to be disappointed that somebody didn't have your troubles, but I was. "Does he take an interest in you?"

He got that glare that he sometimes got and stared around at the field and the woods. "Sure he does," he said.

But something was wrong or he wouldn't have indentured himself to Laydon. "Did you run away, Weetoppin?"

He didn't say anything. Then he said, "Father know why I go."

He wasn't going to tell me any more. "Well, I'll tell you, Weetoppin, someday I'm going to be big. And when he tries to give me a whipping, I'm going to pick up a hoe and bust him with it."

That was when Laydon popped out of the ground. He stood there looking down at us. I held my breath—had he heard me?

But he hadn't. "You haven't got very far along, have you boys? Been talking. They say a boy is worth half a man and two boys aren't worth anything at all. I guess what they say is right. I'll have to separate you."

I didn't want that, not by a long shot. Me and Weetoppin were finally beginning to get along a little. I swallowed down my feelings. "Sir, Weetoppin hasn't got the hang of it yet. You got to remember that he never did any farm work before. In his village the women do it."

It was a good excuse and I was proud of it. For a

minute, Laydon didn't say anything. We looked at him. I knew he was thinking that he'd better not push Weetoppin too hard at first, for he might get angry and go back to his village. He said, "All right, Richard. But it's your neck. You better see that he gets the hang of it mighty quick or I'll turn both of your backs red." He went to the edge of the woods, picked up a stick, carried it back to where we were, and stuck it in the ground to show how far along we'd got. "I'm going over to Jamestown. When I come back, I want to see that you've weeded a good distance down the line from this stick." He turned and stalked off across the field towards the river, where he kept his skiff tied up.

"He was going to whip us?"

"Oh, he was bound to if I hadn't spoken up so quick." I didn't guess he would have, not on Weetoppin's first day. But I figured I might as well get some credit. "Let's get some weeding done."

So we weeded until I reckoned that Laydon had got across the James to the fort. Then we moved the stick back a hundred feet and went for a swim in the river. It was still a little cold that time of year, but mighty nice after working all day in the hot sun.

On Sunday, Laydon made Weetoppin go to church with us. "That's half the point of it," he said. "The Indians will be far better off if they get a little Christianity in them. It's our Christian duty to see that they learn about our Lord. Maybe then they won't be so quick to kill each other." It didn't seem to me that the English were doing so good on the Christian end of it either, but I figured I'd better not say anything.

But Weetoppin figured that going to church beat weeding tobacco seedlings. Besides, he got to put on a clean shirt and trousers. As we rowed across the river to Jamestown, he kept trying to look in the water to see how grand he looked in English clothes, but the water was too rippled to reflect much. He fell asleep about five minutes into the sermon and stayed asleep, even though I jabbed him in the ribs from time to time. I guess it was all a mystery to him. To tell the truth, a lot of it was a mystery to me too, but I knew better than to fall asleep—though the temptation was mighty strong sometimes.

I noticed a few people giving us looks as we came out of church. There had been Indians in church before, but people were always curious about any new ones. They wanted to know who brought them and why they were living with Englishmen. So it didn't surprise me any when we came out of church to see Henry Spofford come strolling up to us. He was a tall man with long black hair, dressed up mighty grand in big black boots, a ruffled shirt, and a wide hat with a feather in it. Laydon bowed his head a little and I bowed too, but Weetoppin just stared at Spofford in those grand clothes. I don't guess he'd ever seen anything like them. I had, for Henry Spofford always dressed up grand for church. "I see you've got yourself an Indian boy, Laydon," he said.

"I caught him stealing a hoe. We worked out a deal. He's going to stay with me. Although I don't know as he's

going to be of any more use than the boy I already have."
No credit to me for any of it. It made me mad but I
couldn't say anything.

"You've indentured him, the Indian?" Spofford wasn't
looking at Laydon, but at Susan. There were a couple of
patches on Susan's dress, but she had pressed it neat for
church and had put some flowers in her hat. She looked
real nice. I'd much rather look at her than at Laydon.

"I guess you could call it that. He's working for me,
anyway."

"Why'd his parents let him go?" Spofford asked.

"Some kind of trouble back in the village."

Spofford looked at Laydon and nodded. "If he's just
working for you, that's one thing. If you mean it as an
indenture, Laydon, you'd better get it in writing. You
need something on paper in case questions come up. In
case you need to sell the indenture or something like
that."

"Oh, I don't know as I need to go to all that trouble
with an Indian. Different with an English servant."

"It's your business," Spofford shrugged. He looked at
Susan again. "Your girl has grown up considerable since
the last time I noticed."

Susan blushed. "I'm 18, sir," she said.

"So I see," Spofford said. "I reckon your indenture'll
be up soon."

Susan went on blushing. "In two years, sir."

"And what'll you do then?"

Susan shook her head in order to get herself to stop

blushing. "I don't know, sir. I haven't thought about it."

"You ought to give it some thought," he said. "Good morning, then." He turned and left, and we walked down to the river, climbed into the skiff, and rowed back across the James. All the time I was rowing, I was thinking: You needed something in writing for an indenture. It had to be in writing. That meant that Laydon must have got a piece of paper from somebody—the governor, most likely—saying that I was indentured to him. He must have, for how could he prove I belonged to him otherwise? Why hadn't I thought of that before? I'd just gone along taking Laydon's word for it that nothing was written down, that my indenture wouldn't be up until I was grown. It had made some kind of sense. But maybe it wasn't that way at all. Maybe it was written down somewhere when I was supposed to be free from him. And if there was a paper, it had to be in the house somewhere. That was certain.

Chapter 4

Two days later we were working in the tobacco field as usual, when suddenly an Indian came striding out of the woods along the river. We jumped up from where we'd been on our knees weeding. "It's my father," Weetoppin said. "I figured he come."

"How'd you figure that?"

"People see me in church. Indians bound to find out real quick."

Weetoppin's father was tall and dressed in a loincloth. The sun glinted off of his yellow-brown chest. He wore his hair just like Weetoppin's—shaved off on one side of his head and hanging down on the other. He looked mighty strong and dangerous to me. Was he going to take Weetoppin back? I wondered if I ought to make a run for it up to the house to warn Laydon. But I didn't run, for I knew that Weetoppin's father would be on me in a minute. Besides, I was mighty curious, so I stood there and waited.

The Indian strode across the tobacco field like he owned it—which maybe he did once. He didn't look left and he didn't look right, but he kept coming steadily toward us. We watched him keep coming until he was standing right over us, looking down. He was mighty big, all right. Weetoppin was going to be big when he grew up.

For a minute he didn't say anything but stared down at his son. There was nothing much on his face. I couldn't tell if he was sore at Weetoppin for running away, or sorrowful, or what. I wished I knew what it was all about. I kept looking at Weetoppin, and I guess he knew that, for he didn't look back at me.

Then his father said something in Algonquian—the Powhatan tribes were all Algonquians. I could understand a few words of the language but not very much of it.

Weetoppin didn't say anything. He just stared up at his father like he knew he'd done something wrong but wasn't going to apologize for it. Then he answered in Algonquian. His father grunted and strode off towards the house. I was all-fired curious; that's a fact. I figured I had a right to ask: "What does he want?"

Weetoppin didn't say anything.

"Come on, Weetoppin, I'll find out sooner or later."

Weetoppin still didn't say anything.

"Is he going to make you go home?"

"No." He seemed pretty sure of that.

"What's he want from Laydon?"

He gave me that hard look. "Don't know, Richard, I told you, don't know." Then he looked off at the trees. Whatever it was, it was serious, that much I could figure out. So I dropped it. I looked back toward the house. Weetoppin's father had disappeared inside. "We better get to work," I said. "Laydon's sure to come out soon."

I knelt down and began weeding, and in a minute Weetoppin was weeding too. There was nothing much on his face—sadness, if anything. About a half-hour later, Weetoppin's father and Laydon came out of the house and started through the field toward us. Weetoppin's father had a blanket slung over his shoulder and was carrying a metal hatchet. The two men came up to us. We stopped weeding, stood up, and looked at them.

"Weetoppin," Laydon said. "Your father just indentured you to me for that blanket and hatchet. You understand?"

Weetoppin kept his arms folded across his chest and turned his head to look across the field. He wasn't going to look at either of them, and I didn't blame him. Here he'd made a deal with Laydon himself, where he was to get a knife and some other things out of it for himself, and now his father had come along and taken over the deal. It didn't seem fair. But of course, I still didn't know what was behind the whole thing.

"Understand, Weetoppin?" Laydon insisted. He was getting angry. But Weetoppin still wouldn't look at either of them. Suddenly, his father grabbed him by the shoulder and gave him a shake. "You hear, Weetoppin? You work for this English."

Laydon reached in under his shirt and pulled out a piece of paper. He held it up where we could both see it. There was writing on it. Down at the bottom was a little drawing of a fish with a line going through it at an angle, meaning an arrow or a spear stuck into it. Indians couldn't write English any more than I could, so they would sign treaties and such with a little drawing that had to do with their names. I reckoned Weetoppin's father was called Fishcatcher or Spearfisher or something. So it was official: Weetoppin was indentured just like me. Of course it didn't mean much to indenture an Indian—they could always run off.

But seeing that paper made a ray of sunshine go through me. So it was true: If you indentured somebody, there was bound to be a paper about it. Laydon *must* have an indenture paper for me too. But where? In the house somewhere, that was certain. I was bound and determined to find it. I was as sure as I could be that it said when my time would be up. Otherwise why would Laydon be so set on keeping it hidden and saying that there wasn't any such paper? Oh, it had to be somewhere. I just *had* to find it.

Anyway, it surprised me a good deal that Fishcatcher or whatever his name was had indentured his own son to an Englishman. It wasn't like the Indians. They usually went pretty easy on their kids, as far as I could see. They used to come up to the fort a lot when Governor Dale was in charge, before Governor Argyll took over and said the Indians wasn't to visit without permission. The Indians let the children run around unhindered. Like the way it was with Pocahontas when she was a girl. Of course she was the daughter of the big king Powhatan and could do as she pleased, but even so. She would come up to Jamestown naked as a jay, like all Indian kids. She'd call the boys out to play with her, and show them how to turn cartwheels—just go wheeling around the village without asking anybody's leave. Or so they told me—I was too young to remember. We English kids wouldn't dare do anything like that, not without asking somebody's leave. Especially naked. We were expected to rule ourselves better than that. But the Indian children were allowed to be more unruly, and their folks would just smile about it.

So it was mighty surprising for Weetoppin to get sold off as a servant by his father. As much as the English planters wanted Indians to work the tobacco fields for them and were ready to pay good, the Indians wouldn't sell their children for it. They thought too much of them. They didn't want them picking up English ways, either—they thought too much of their own ways. You would have thought they'd want to pick up our ways, like having snug houses to live in and tables to eat on. And raising cows, hogs, and chickens for meat instead of having to hunt deer and go hungry when the corn ran out in the spring. You'd have thought they'd want to take our God too. It was clear that their gods weren't much compared to our Lord. Anyone could see that. Everybody said that the Lord wanted to get rid of the Indians so we could have the land here in Virginia and turn it into Christian country. That's why the Indians dropped like flies from our diseases like measles and smallpox, and the English didn't—well, they didn't a lot of the time. If the Indians had any sense they'd come over to our side, and maybe the Lord would let them live when they got one of our diseases. But they didn't. They liked their own ways best.

That's natural, I figured. But still, it didn't do the Indians any good.

Anyway, it wasn't like the Indians to indenture one of their own children, and I was mighty curious as to why it had happened to Weetoppin. I knew it wasn't polite to pry into other people's business. So for a while there—after Weetoppin's father strode off to where he'd tied up his canoe, and Laydon had gone back to the house, and we were alone once more—I tried like the devil to keep my mouth shut and not ask. It was blame hard. I kept telling myself, "Richard, it's none of your business." But my curiosity wouldn't go away. I'd set myself to thinking about something else—like why were the leaves green and the sky blue and not the other way around? And about three minutes later, Weetoppin would come popping back into my mind again. Finally I saw that I'd never be able to hold out. I was bound to ask sooner or later. I decided I might as well get it over with instead of worrying about it the rest of the day. So I eased into it. "Weetoppin, how come the Indians don't like their kids to be raised up among the English? I would have thought they'd want them to learn about raising hogs and chickens and going to our church where they'd be safe from measles."

"English ways no good. Work too hard."

"Well, yes. But you don't get anywhere without hard work. I mean Laydon says he's going to be rich, but he has to work hard if he wants to be."

"Indian ways better," Weetoppin said. He was being stubborn, but he'd trapped himself.

"All right, then how come your father indentured you to Laydon?"

He didn't say anything.

"Come on, you might as well tell me. I'll find out sooner or later. Laydon knows, I'll be bound."

"No," he said.

"I thought we were supposed to be friends."

He clenched his lips.

"I bet you got into trouble at home. I bet you did something awful and can't stay there anymore."

He gave me his hard look again. "I didn't do nothing."

"Well, that makes it clear enough that you *did* do something."

He didn't answer but went on hoeing, keeping his eyes on the head of the hoe scratching at the weeds between the lines of tobacco plants. The plants were bigger now and there wasn't much risk of breaking them with the hoe. I knew I was right: He'd done something. But he wasn't going to tell me, that was certain. We went along working.

When the sun was overhead, Susan banged the fireplace poker on the water barrel by the front door. We went up to the house for noonday dinner. Laydon wasn't there, and I was mighty glad. It was a real nice place when he wasn't around and me and Susan and Weetoppin could sit in the coolness of the house and eat our dinners and talk about things. "Where'd he go?" I asked.

"He had to go over to Jamestown for a muster. The governor's sending some men up the river to scout around the Indian villages for corn."

"I thought we were finally growing enough corn for ourselves."

"We probably are. But the governor wants to be on the safe side."

"Indians don't have no spare corn," Weetoppin said.

Susan shrugged. "If they find any, they'll make the Indians trade."

"Maybe Indians fight. Maybe kill Laydon."

"Shusshh, Weetoppin," Susan said. "Don't let anyone hear you say things like that. You'll get yourself into a lot of trouble."

"Don't care," he said.

I liked the way the sun coming through the window shone on Susan's yellow hair. "Susan," I said, "You wouldn't mind if Laydon got killed in a fight, would you?"

"I'm not going to answer such a question. It's not Christian to think such things."

"Indians should kill all the English," Weetoppin said.

"What about me and Susan? Would you like it if they killed us too?"

Weetoppin frowned and looked out the window. "Sure," he said. "Kill all the English."

"You're just talking," I said. "You wouldn't want us to get killed."

"All right," Susan said mighty sharp. " I don't want to hear any more of this from you two boys. Now sit down and eat your dinners." She banged a wooden platter of cornbread on the table and we sat down to eat.

By and by, I began to think of what a nice day it was

for taking a swim. "Susan, did he say when he was coming back?"

"No. He said you boys were to work on rooting out the stumps nearest the house." That was tough work. Generally speaking, when anyone set about clearing land in order to grow tobacco, they sawed off the trees a couple feet up from the ground and then burned the stumps to get rid of them. The ashes were good for the soil too. A new field was always filled with tree stumps of different sizes sticking up everywhere. When they were growing corn, though, it didn't much matter about the stumps. But with tobacco bringing in so much money, you wanted every inch of land you could get. You could grow two or three tobacco plants in the space that a tree stump took, so it was worth grubbing the stumps out. But it was mighty hard work. We had to dig a trench all around the stump, hack off the roots, and then try to pry the stump out. That was the worst part, for there was usually a tap root growing straight down from the bottom of the stump, maybe two or three feet deep. Grubbing out stumps would keep us real busy while Laydon was gone— that was the whole point of it.

"If they're scouting Indian villages upriver they'll be gone overnight," I reckoned.

Susan shrugged. "I wouldn't count on it."

"They can't go very far upriver and get back before nightfall."

She looked at me. "I'd make sure you're covered with sweat and dirt when he comes back, not looking clean with your hair slicked back like you just got out of the river."

I blushed. "I didn't say we were going swimming."

"You didn't have to."

After dinner we got a couple of grub hoes out of the shed and went out to the tobacco field, looking for the smallest stump we could find. "Listen, Weetoppin, where do you think they've gone?"

He shrugged. "Don't know. Maybe Appamattuc village. They might have corn."

"That's thirty or forty miles upriver," I said. "It'll take them two days to get there and back. He won't be back today. Let's get a start on this stump so we have something to show. Then we'll go for a swim."

He grunted. Being as contrary as he was, Weetoppin wasn't ever likely to agree with me about anything. He'd just grunt instead—oomph. It was as close as he would come to saying yes.

So we grubbed away at the stump for a while, cutting a trench around it a couple of feet from the base. But something else was itching and scratching at me. So when we'd sweated over that stump and got a trench cut two feet deep all around it, I dropped my hoe. "I'm going to tell Susan we're going swimming," I said, "so she can bang on the water barrel if he comes back."

I went up to the house and into the coolness of it. Susan was sewing a button that had come loose on one of Laydon's shirts. "Susan," I said, "How come Laydon took the trouble of writing out an indenture paper for Weetoppin when he didn't bother with one for me?"

"How do you know he didn't?"

"He says he didn't. He says it was never spelled out how long I had to stay his servant. He says I have to be indentured until I'm a grownup and that it's up to him to decide when that is."

"I know he says that," Susan said. "He's said it often enough."

"You were a girl when you came over. How come you have a regular indenture paper?"

"I agreed to come to Virginia. I wanted to come. You know how it was—my father dead and my mother and me were scrambling around every year to find a new place for ourselves, sleeping on straw in barns and eating old bread and cheese if we were lucky. Everybody said we could make a new life for ourselves in Virginia—could grow tobacco and get rich. They didn't say anything about the starving times and the sickness and getting whipped by your master whenever he felt like it. So I indentured myself."

"Laydon doesn't whip you," I said.

"He did at first, when I was 13 and had just come over. But then I grew a little. One day I was cutting corn off the cob to make a stew with milk. The knife slipped and I knocked over the milk pitcher. Before I knew what hit me, he had come around with his belt and slashed me across the face. I was holding the knife in my hand. I swung around and jabbed it at his gut. I don't know what made me do it, for I was always a peaceable girl. But I did it. I would have sliced him wide open if he hadn't been quick as lightning and jumped back. He fell over a chair

43

and was lying there on the ground. I said, "If you ever hit me again I'll put this knife into you." I was trembling so hard I could hardly talk, but he saw I meant it and never hit me again."

"I wish I dared do something like that," I said.

"You will," she said. "You aren't big enough yet."

I thought for a minute. "What're you going to do when your indenture is up?"

"Get married. That's the only way I'll ever have land. There are a half-dozen men in Virginia for every woman. I can pick and choose. Get somebody who's got a plantation started already." Her eyes got kind of dreamy and she looked out across the field. "I'll have my own house and servants to work for me instead of being one myself. That's what I'm going to do. And you can come and visit me, Richard, and we'll talk about old times."

"First I have to get free of Laydon. Susan, I just know that he's got a paper about my indenture somewhere."

"How do you reckon that?"

"At church the other day, Henry Spofford told Laydon that he ought to get a paper indenture on Weetoppin so as to make it legal. And that's what Laydon did when Weetoppin's father showed up. If he needs a paper for Weetoppin, he needs a paper for me. It's got to be around here somewhere."

Susan thought about it. "Well, if he's got it, I don't know where it is."

"I'm going to find it," I said. "See if you can think of where he might have hidden it."

"I'll try," she said. "but I can't think of anyplace right offhand."

"I'll find it," I said. "Anyway, we're going swimming."

"Don't say I didn't warn you. He'll whip you for sure if he catches you."

I turned to go outside again. Then I stopped and turned back. "Susan, you were here when Weetoppin's father was bargaining with Laydon. Did he say why he was willing to indenture his own son?"

She looked surprised. "Weetoppin didn't tell you?"

"No. I asked him, but he wouldn't say."

"I'm surprised. I figured with you and him being friendly, he would have told you."

"Well, he didn't."

"He can't go home." She took a breath. "He killed another Indian boy."

Chapter 5

It was a shock, all right, to learn that Weetoppin had killed somebody. Killing wasn't uncommon around Virginia: Indians killed us, we killed Indians, Indians killed other Indians, and sometimes the governor would hang somebody for something. One governor even tortured to death a couple of men who'd run off to the Indians and got caught again. There was a lot more killing out here in Virginia than I ever saw in London. Hanging, we had that back home, and I guess there was a murder from time to time. But I never saw anybody killed, nor knew of any killings, except for murderers and thieves and such who got hung.

So it wasn't any surprise that somebody had killed somebody else. The shock was that it was Weetoppin. *Men* killed people, not boys. Oh, maybe I'd have understood it if Weetoppin had been in some Indian battle—if his village had got attacked and he'd grabbed up a bow and shot one of the enemy. I could have understood something like that. But not shooting a boy from his own village. Here I'd been working with Weetoppin 12 hours a day, eating with him, going swimming with him, sleeping in the same bed with him.

Hardly ever apart for more than two minutes at a time. And it turned out that he was a murderer. I'd never known a murderer, never even seen one except dangling from a rope in Tyburn, in London. And here I was sleeping in the same bed with one. It gave me a mighty strange feeling, all right.

I wondered—ought I have a murderer for a friend? Laydon knew about it, and it didn't bother him. It didn't seem to bother Susan either. Why should it bother me? How did I feel about Weetoppin now that I knew? Well, I knew that I felt a little different. He wasn't exactly the same person I thought he was before. He'd changed. It seemed somehow that he had an important secret that I wasn't in on. He'd had something happen to him that I hadn't, and wasn't ever likely to either. To tell the truth, I was a little jealous of him. It surprised me, but I was. Not that I wanted to kill anybody—well, Laydon sometimes, I guess—but probably not really even him. But still, something big had happened to Weetoppin and nothing big had happened to me.

Of course I didn't know what it was all about. Maybe it had just been some accident—he was wrestling with the kid and banged his head on a rock by accident. Something that could have happened to anybody.

And suppose I'd killed Weetoppin the day that he stole the hoe and I cornered him by the marsh? I tried to think back. There he was, sprawled out on the ground, and there I was, standing over him with the knife. I could see it all in my mind clear enough. But I couldn't remember if I meant to drop down to my knees and ram the knife into his gut like Susan almost did to Laydon. Was I planning on doing it before Laydon stopped me? I couldn't remember. It had all happened too fast.

What did Weetoppin remember about murdering that boy? I was bound I'd find out. I walked across the field to collect him and we set off for the river. It was a nice feeling, being free for a change. We sauntered along, smelling the air, listening to the wind rustle in the leaves, watching the birds flash through the trees—brown, red, blue, even some yellow ones. It was all mighty pretty when you didn't have to work and could enjoy it. "If we were rich, Weetoppin, we could have fun like this all the time."

"Indians don't need to be rich to have fun. English people work too much. Indians only work when they need to."

I had to grant that there was something to that. The Indians wanted our cloth, metal tools, and metal pots, but they didn't want much else of ours. They were content with their skin-covered lodges and were happy with their own gods. Anyway, I was enjoying myself too much to get into an argument about it. We got to the riverbank, stripped, and slid down the muddy bank into the water. Being as it was June, the water was pretty warm. Oh my, it felt good just to float along there on our backs, looking up at the white fluffy clouds drifting along across the blue sky. I knew we couldn't stay too long, though, for we'd have to make enough headway on that stump to convince Laydon that we'd been sweating away at it the whole time he was gone. But it was too nice to leave right away, so we paddled around for a while.

Then suddenly I heard a distant splash. I raised my head up. There, coming across the river, was the skiff. We leaped out of the water, grabbed our clothes, and raced naked back through the woods and across the field to the stump. We dressed as quick as we could, and when Laydon came striding out of the woods we were swinging those grub hoes fast and furious and making the dirt fly.

Had he seen us? He'd been pretty far off when I spotted the boat. He might have been too busy with the oars to notice us. He came across the field straight toward us, not veering right or left, like a wolf going for a deer. We went on grubbing at the dirt like we didn't have anything on our minds but getting that stump out. He strode up to us. I looked up at him. "We're doing pretty good on this stump, sir." I pointed to the trench. "Look."

He gave it a quick glance. He nodded, "Didn't expect me back so soon, did you, Richard?"

"We weren't expecting anything," I said, trying to think of how to twist out of it. "We've been hacking away at this stump all afternoon. See how much we've got done."

Suddenly he reached over and grabbed my hair. "Wet," he said. He gave my head a shake by the hair. It hurt.

"We're covered with sweat," I said.

He gave my head another shake. "I never saw hair that could sweat that much."

He was still hanging onto my hair and I tried to pull loose. "I didn't say it was all sweat. A little bit ago we went up to the house and ladled some water over ourselves to cool down." My eyes were beginning to sting from having my hair pulled.

He got tired of pulling my hair and let go. "I might have believed that if I hadn't seen a couple of boys jump out of the water as I was coming across." He looked at Weetoppin. "Who's first?"

"Don't you touch me!" Weetoppin shouted.

"What?" Laydon yelled. He reached out and whacked Weetoppin across the face with the back of his hand.

Weetoppin staggered back, but he didn't fall. A trickle of blood rolled down his lip. "I'll kill you!" he shouted.

Laydon leaped for Weetoppin. He grabbed Weetoppin by the braid and jerked him toward himself. Weetoppin kicked out, trying to catch Laydon in the calf. Laydon slapped him hard across the face, snapping Weetoppin's head back. Weetoppin stood there blinking and trying to make his face still. "I'll kill you," he whispered.

"You say that once more and we'll see who kills who." Laydon pulled his belt out of his trousers, took Weetoppin's head under one arm and began lashing him across the back with the belt, smack, smack, smack. The smacks kept coming as steady as church bells. I couldn't see Weetoppin's face, but his body was dead still. Not twisting or wriggling, he was holding himself still and taking it. It would be my turn next. I felt just awful waiting for it, for there wasn't a thing I could do. I

50

couldn't run, for there was nobody to run to, and they'd catch me soon enough anyway. If a servant ran away they were allowed to add a couple of years to your indenture and whip you as much as they pleased. So I stood there waiting with that heavy feeling inside. I made up my mind that I wouldn't wriggle either.

Finally, Laydon decided he'd given Weetoppin enough. He shoved him away. Weetoppin fell onto the ground and lay there on his stomach. His back was cut in two or three places and blood was seeping onto his skin.

"Now you, Richard. Like as not it was your idea in the first place."

"Sir," I started to say, but then I remembered about not wriggling and shut my mouth. He grabbed my head under his arm the way he'd done Weetoppin, and then the smacks came, one after the next, the shocking sting spreading through me and fading before the next one came. I put my lower lip between my teeth so as not to cry, bit into it so hard I could taste the blood, and tried to hold myself still the way Weetoppin had done. But sometimes the stings would be so bad I couldn't help myself and my legs would jerk.

Finally Laydon was done. He shoved me down beside Weetoppin and went off to the house, looping his belt back into his trousers. We lay there awhile, waiting for the pain to die down a little and for our strength to come back. Finally I sat up. "Weetoppin, are you all right?"

He sat up and stared at the house. "Someday I gonna kill him. Someday."

I looked at Weetoppin and thought maybe he would. If he'd already killed one person, maybe he could do it again. "Let's go down to the river and wash ourselves up some," I said. "I did it before. It'll heal better if you get the dirt out of the cuts. Laydon won't bother us any more today. He's got it out of himself for now."

We went down to the river and washed up. Weetoppin knew about a plant that was supposed to be good for cuts like this. It was some kind of Indian medicine. And I'm blamed if it didn't ease down the pain a little. Then we sat on the bank watching the river go by, trying not to think about how much our backs hurt, and I got into the whole thing. "Weetoppin, I know why you ran away from your village."

He looked at me and then looked away again.

"You killed some boy."

He looked at me again. "Who told you?"

"Susan did. Your father told Laydon and she heard it."

He looked away across the river, like he was seeing something that wasn't there. "I didn't mean to. I was just trying to scare him."

I could see that he was willing to talk about it—that he *wanted* to talk about it. "What'd he do to you?"

He didn't say anything for a minute. He wanted to talk about it, but it was a struggle. "He was my best friend. We was like brothers. Old friends from when we were babies." Then he looked ashamed and stopped.

"What happened?" I said to encourage him.

"He kept saying things to me. I told him to stop. He wouldn't stop."

"What things?"

He took a deep breath. "My mother, she got burned in a fire—whole side of her was crippled. Face, arm, leg. My friend, he teased me. Was saying, 'Your mother, she don't look so good. Your mother, she got crooked arm.' I say, 'Don't say those things or I kill you.' He won't stop. One day we was hunting birds. He say, 'You better shoot good, bring home bird for cripple arm.' I got mad. I was going to scare him. I swung around and aimed my bow, and before I knew what I was doing I let the arrow go. Went straight into his heart. He looked at me surprised and died."

He stopped talking again, and for the first time since I had known him I thought he was going to cry. I felt mighty bad for him. "How'd you feel when you saw he was dead?"

He shook his head to get the picture out of his eyes. "I felt like I was going to die myself. I wish I had died. Easier to be dead than feel like this."

"You still feel bad about it?"

He looked at me. "Always. I never feel good again, ever."

"So that's why you had to leave?"

"Boy's father told chief I had to be killed. They make you lay your head on a rock, and chief, he smashes it with a club. That night my father took me out to the woods and told me to run. I hid in the woods for three days. They was all looking for me. Didn't have nothing to eat for three days. Didn't have time to stop. Figured I steal some food from the English. Indians wouldn't chase me to English village. Didn't see no food but saw the hoe. Figured I could trade it for food."

"So that's why you was so all-fired hungry that day," I reckoned.

"Could of eat a dog. Saw all that food and figured I better stay here. Can't go home no more, safe from Indians here. English save me from my own people."

He had told me something that was hard for him to tell. I decided I'd tell him something too. But it wasn't so hard for me to tell as it was for him. I hadn't done anything to be ashamed of, although to tell the truth I was ashamed of it. I didn't know why, but I was. "At least you had a father. I didn't have anybody to take an interest in me. I don't know what happened to my mother and father. Maybe they decided they didn't want me and stuck me in some orphanage. Maybe they died. I hope they died. It's a bad thing to hope somebody died, but I hate thinking that they didn't want me and just shoved me away from them."

"What means orphanage?"

"That's a place where they put kids who don't have a mother or a father. I don't remember much of it. All I can remember is some big room with a lot of little kids sleeping on straw ticks. The first thing I really remember is begging on the streets of London. We had a gang. Mostly older kids—10, 11, 12 years old. They used to send me out to beg because I was so young and could get people's sympathy. They stole from shops. Stole whatever they could. At night we met under a bridge and shared. Made a fire and cooked whatever we had. The older boys looked after me, saw to it I had my share. But they were always mighty hungry too and didn't give me any more than my share. Slept on the Common in good weather. Slept in stables when we could sneak into them during bad weather."

"Then two of the boys got caught stealing some bread from a shop. All of us went to Tyburn to see them be hanged. They shouted down from the scaffold that being hanged wasn't anything, that they weren't scared, and that our turn would come soon enough. We shouted back at them that we'd have a toast to them that night when we were drinking our beer and eating our bread and sausages, but it was all lies, for none of us was feeling too cheerful. When we saw those boys, who weren't more than 12 or 13, jerking and kicking at the end of those ropes, we got mighty quiet and slunk off. The gang kind of broke up after that."

"It wasn't long after that when some men scooped me off the street where I was begging, carried me across the river to Southwark, and shipped me over here." I looked at Weetoppin. "At least you had a father."

Chapter 6

After that, me and Weetoppin were solid friends. We'd been friendly, slept in the same bed, worked together all day long. But before, he was always a little cautious with me. Didn't talk about himself a whole lot. I still wouldn't call him a chatterbox, but he got to be more talky. It was the way I had hoped it would be all along—somebody to pass the time with when there was 12 hours of hoeing or picking bugs off of leaves to be done.

It got into July. The tobacco was pretty high. From now until September, all four of us would be going at it hot and heavy. There were always weeds to hoe between the rows of tobacco plants. But now there were the bugs to take care of too. Lots of them. We had to go down the rows, look over each plant real careful, take the bugs off, and squash them. I couldn't understand how there could be so many bugs in the world. One day we'd squash hundreds of them, thousands maybe, and the next day there'd be thousands more. You'd have thought the day would come when they were all squashed up, but they never were. They just kept on coming. What with making all those bugs, I don't see how the Lord had any time left over for anything else.

Oh, we were going to be mighty busy for the next few weeks. In September we'd have to pick the leaves and hang them in the tobacco barn to cure. Then we'd have to pack them into hogsheads and cart them across to Jamestown to the tobacco ships that piled up around then. Susan grumbled about the work a good deal. She would much rather be in the house, where it was cool and she could sit down and rest from time to time instead of bending her back over the tobacco plants in the hot sun. When her indenture was up, she said, she was going to have lots of servants and would never work in the fields again. Of course, she didn't say any of this when Laydon could hear it.

But Laydon was pretty cheerful about it all. The crop was coming in pretty good. He could see where he was going to have a nice profit if his luck held—if we didn't get a long dry spell or a hailstorm smashing down the plants. He kept a sharp eye on us, but he wasn't laying into us with his tongue all day long the way he usually did.

Besides, having him out there in the field with us gave me the chance I'd been wanting for weeks—the chance to find where he'd hid my indenture paper. It wasn't easy for me to find excuses to slip into the house but I kept my mind on it, and from time to time I came up with something. For one thing, somebody had to go up to the house for water now and again. We all wanted to do it, for it made a change from bending over the tobacco plants. I tried to make sure my turn came when we were working way down from the house, at the far end of the field. I'd go up to the house, fill the jug at the water barrel, take a quick look to see if Laydon was watching, and then dash into the house and start rummaging around. The house wasn't but one big room with a fireplace at one end and a door at the other. Upstairs was a loft, with the roof slanting down on both sides and a window at each end. A shed was attached to the back of the house, where we stored firewood and kept milk to stay cool. In real bad weather, we brought the cow and the chickens in there too.

Laydon's bed was to one side of the big room, near the fireplace in the winter for warmth, near the door in the summer for coolness. I rummaged all through his bed, even untied the mattress and reached down inside to feel around in the straw. Nothing there. I looked up the chimney to see if he hadn't hid an iron box up there somewhere. Nothing. One day I even slid under the house to see if he hadn't rolled up my indenture paper and tucked it behind a beam. Nothing there either. Searching under the house took longer than I planned, and Laydon got suspicious. "What took you so long getting water, Richard?"

"One of the chickens got into the house and was making a mess. I couldn't catch the blame thing."

"You should have taken a broom and run it out."

"I thought of it, finally, sir. Then I had to clean up after it."

He was still suspicious. "What's that mud all over your shirt?"

58

"When I finally shooed the chicken into the yard, I got my feet tangled up in the broom and fell down right there by the water barrel, where it's muddy."

He eyed me. "You been up to something, Richard. Stealing food I shouldn't wonder."

"I wouldn't think of doing anything like that, sir." Of course, whoever went up for water was certain to slip into the house and snatch a piece of cornbread, or something, out of the cupboard. Or scoop a finger around in the jam pot, if there was any jam.

"No, of course you wouldn't, Richard," Laydon said. But he let it go. He'd rather think about how much money he was going to make off his tobacco.

Besides, he had something else on his mind. Back in London, the Company had decided to set up in Virginia what they were going to call the House of Burgesses. I didn't have any idea what that meant and was curious. But I didn't have to ask to find out, for Laydon was full of it and couldn't stop talking about it. He was bound and determined he was going to be in this House of Burgesses. It got so that we hardly sat down to dinner and started shoveling in the cornbread and pork before he started in on it. "You three are too ignorant to understand what it means. Why, none of you can even read or write your names. How could you possibly understand?"

"I can read," Susan Cooper said. "I can read the Bible."

"Well, you can't read much. I've seen you. Spell out the words a little is all you can do. Whereas I can read a page straight out and write a letter too."

"I could read if somebody would teach me," I said.

"It isn't as easy as you think, Richard," Laydon said. "Not everybody's up to it, especially someone like you who was dragged off the streets and hadn't much brains to start with. So I'm bound to be elected to the House of Burgesses. They need men who can read and write. We're going to be running things out here in Virginia soon enough. It's going to be like our own Parliament here. Vote on things, decide this or that."

"What sort of things?" I said. This was about the 15th time I'd heard it all, and I was tired of it.

"Oh, the usual sorts of things that have to be decided."

"Like what?"

"Don't be so impertinent, Richard, or you'll get something you're not looking for. Why, we'll decide all sorts of things. Important things."

"Like whether it rains or shines," Susan said. "That's real important." She had got bored with it too.

Laydon smacked his hand down on the table. "I'm not above giving you a whipping, either. Keep it in mind."

I could see that he was losing his temper and was about to lay into somebody, and I came up with something polite to say. "I thought the governor decided things, sir."

"Oh, he does. But we'll help. It's going to be a glorious thing. Where else in the world do ordinary people get in on the government and help decide things?" He glared around and slapped his hand on the table

60

again. "Nowhere, that's where. But right here in Virginia we're going to have this House of Burgesses, and have a say in things."

It was like that all the time. I was sick of it. Oh, I could see where there would be some value in this House of Burgesses. Most places, people didn't have any say in what the government did. Not back in England they didn't, anyway. The king decided most everything, and the dukes and earls decided the rest. You had to do what they said or they'd chop your head off, or hang you at Tyburn, like they did those boys in our gang. Of course there was Parliament, but only rich people who owned half a county could get into Parliament. I didn't know that myself, for I didn't know much about anything, but that's what others said about it. You'd hear the men after church in Jamestown going on about it. They were always talking about what Parliament had done, or was going to do, or might have done if this or that was the case. Laydon grumbled about Parliament a good deal too. Didn't grumble about King James, though. He didn't dare. But grumbling about Parliament was safe enough, I reckoned, for everybody did it.

Maybe it was different in someplace like China or Persia. I didn't know anything about those places, except that they were a long way off, and maybe just made-up places, for all I knew. But in the places I knew about, like London and Virginia, the ordinary people didn't have any say in things. It was all run by the ones God had put at the top. So I could see where this House of Burgesses might be a good thing, if anything Laydon had said about it was true—give ordinary people a say in things.

Of course, when it got down to the details, I could see that this House of Burgesses wasn't going to have the whole say, not by far. The governor would have the last word, and the Company back in London would have an even laster word, for they had to approve what was done out here. As far as that went, most of us ordinary people were left out altogether. Only those who paid taxes would vote. That left all of us servants out—we weren't to have a say, for we didn't even have a say in our own lives.

Oh, where was that indenture paper? I'd looked and looked and couldn't find it anywhere. Susan had looked too, and she couldn't find it either. It was on my mind a lot, and I talked to her about it whenever I could, like when we happened to be picking bugs at one end of a row while the others were at the other end. "It's got to be somewhere, blame it."

"Maybe Laydon isn't lying about it, Richard. Maybe there never was a paper."

"Don't say that, Susan. There has to be a paper. There always is."

"Richard, I don't mean to be hard on you, but maybe this time there wasn't. You were hardly more than a baby—"

"I was six."

"All right, a child. You weren't any use to anybody; they were glad to find somebody who'd take you off their hands."

"The governor would have done it the right way."

"Maybe it wasn't the governor. The Company was picking people like you off the streets—orphans and beggars and such—because the English government wanted to get rid of you. You weren't anything but a nuisance. There were too many people in England anyway. Nobody in England wanted people like you."

"Nobody wanted *me*, that's certain. Nobody ever wanted me."

"Laydon wants you."

"That doesn't cheer me up any."

"Weetoppin wants you, Richard."

"Well, I know that."

"So do I. We all want you."

The whole thing was about to make me cry. *What difference does it make if anybody wants me?* I said to myself. *So long as I've got a warm place to sleep and three meals a day—which I didn't used to have a lot of the time—why does it matter if anyone wants me?* But blame me, it did. I rubbed my eyes. "So who would have indentured me?"

"If you want me to guess, Richard, the English government just told the Virginia Company to go ahead and take any beggars and orphans they wanted. So they just took you. They wanted as many people over here as they could get to settle the countryside. And they knew that half of everybody who came over was likely to die of sickness before they got seasoned. So they had to keep up a steady supply."

That was true. A lot of the ones I came over with and

got to know on the ship died pretty quick, and more of them died later. "But they must have had some kind of papers on us."

"Maybe," she said. "Maybe not. None of you were very important to anybody except if they could indenture you out and make some money on you. Remember, it cost them a good deal for your passage over. The idea was to sell your indentures when you got here."

"Well then, they must have sold me and got some paper on me."

She shook her head. "Not according to Laydon. He says he didn't pay anything for you. The older ones, 10, 12 years old, they were of some use and could have been sold. But not a 6-year-old. They just gave you to whoever would take you."

"Laydon says he didn't want me. Said the governor made a bunch of them draw lots and he got stuck."

She sighed. "Who knows what the truth is? Richard, you've got to stop worrying about that paper so much. You'll worry yourself to death. You've looked and I've looked. It isn't in the house. Where else could it be?"

I clenched my teeth. "It's got to be somewhere. I'm not going to forget about it."

And then I had some luck. Down toward the end of July, that House of Burgesses got going. Laydon was chosen for it, just like he said he would be. It meant he would go off to Jamestown for days, maybe even a week or two, and I'd have a free hand to search for that paper.

As soon as Laydon left on the first day, I told Susan and Weetoppin that they'd have to do my share of hoeing and squashing bugs for a while, while I went back up to the house. For two hours I searched. I looked everywhere. I pulled the woodpile apart and didn't find anything, had to stack it all up again. Next, I went over the tobacco shed, every inch of it. I didn't find anything. After a couple hours, I quit and went back to the tobacco field, was feeling mighty discouraged and low in my mind. Susan looked at me, but she didn't say anything.

I went on feeling low all day and night. Susan and Weetoppin knew what it was, but Laydon didn't notice. He came rolling in from Jamestown late, just as fired up as he could be. He told Susan to make him his supper, and then he made us sit there while he told us all about his trip. Luckily my mind was still on that blame paper, though, so I didn't catch most of it. From what I got, they'd had just a glorious time passing laws about everything they could think of. They had just the finest time. "Of course the governor, he's got to approve it, and so does the Company back in London when they get the news. But they will. They know they can't run everything from over there. They know they've got to let us settle some things here. They know we're bound to work harder at building up the Virginia settlement if we have some say in things and see where it's an advantage to us."

"How many days will it go on, sir?"

"Glad to get rid of me, eh, Richard?"

There wasn't any way to answer that question, so I didn't.

"Keep it in mind that I'll be checking to see how you're getting along." He took a drink of beer. "It won't drag on, I tell you. It's hot as a bake oven in that church where we're meeting. Some have already taken sick. I don't know how long they'll hold out if we don't get a rain to cool things off."

So I was warned. But the very next day, I went back over that house, the woodshed, the tobacco barn, every inch of everything. There wasn't any paper. I went back down to the tobacco field, feeling as low as could be.

Susan looked at me. "Didn't find it, Richard?"

"It isn't there. I looked everywhere. It isn't in the house, nor in any of the sheds."

"Richard, stop worrying about it. You can't go off on your own at your age, anyway."

"Run away to the Indians," Weetoppin said.

"*You* can't even live with the Indians, Weetoppin," I said.

That night, Laydon came home and said that the House of Burgesses was over for now. The heat and sicknesses had got to them. But Laydon was mighty cheerful about it. "It just shows that ordinary people can legislate for themselves when they're allowed."

Chapter 7

A couple mornings later when we were working in the tobacco field, Laydon told Weetoppin to go up to the house for water. Susan was up the row a ways. "Richard, I sent Weetoppin after water on purpose, for I want to talk to you."

That wasn't usual. I straightened up and leaned on the hoe. "Yes, sir."

"Richard, I've been meaning to speak to you about this. You're getting too friendly with Weetoppin."

That surprised me a good deal. "I thought it was the Christian thing to be friendly to others."

"The Indians aren't Christians. They aren't the same as us. They don't count. They'll kill you just as soon as look at you. You got to keep that in mind. Weetoppin may seem friendly now, but turn your back on him and he'll put a knife into you."

"No he won't, sir. I know him."

"I'm telling you, he will. Those Indians are different from us. We had Christian upbringings and know right from wrong. They don't. They're a different kind of people from us. We'll never get along with them. You can't mix the two of us up. It won't work."

"I thought the idea was to turn them into English people, sir."

"Yes, I know. That's what they think in England. But they haven't seen it with their own eyes, like I have. They'd think different if they had. You see any signs of Weetoppin wanting to become English? He doesn't pay the slightest bit of attention in church, but falls asleep the minute he sits down, and he stays asleep the whole time."

It was true. Weetoppin didn't want to become English. He'd said so often enough. "Well, even if he doesn't want to become English, I don't see where Weetoppin's all that different from me."

"He tried to steal that hoe, didn't he? You wouldn't steal anybody's hoe. You got Christian beliefs, even though I'm blamed if I know where you got them, growing up on the streets and sleeping in stables with the horses the way you did. Me, you can understand how I got Christian beliefs. I was raised in a good, prosperous home. We had a stone barn, cattle, sheep, four or five servants. Father read to us from the Bible every morning before breakfast, servants and all. We went to church regular.

"I never would have come to Virginia, but I had two older brothers before me. My father said he liked me as much as any of them, but according to the law, the oldest son got the farm. He sent my other brother, George, to be apprenticed as a law clerk, and he said he'd do the same for me. I tried it. It didn't suit me, scribbling away at a desk until it got too dark to see. Of course, there was all the talk about Virginia. A man could do real well for himself over here, everybody said. Nobody talked much about the sickness and running out of corn and getting murdered by Indians. My father said he'd pay my way over and give me a little something to get started with. He said it was the best he could do for me."

Laydon had never talked to me this much about himself before. It was kind of strange. "So that's how you got the money for this piece of land?" I asked.

"Father didn't have much to give me, but it was enough for this little patch and three servants. But two of them died on me and I was left with Susan until you came along."

"And you got me for nothing, sir."

"That's all you were worth. Nobody wanted you. You were just another mouth to feed."

"But they must have written it down about me somewhere."

He frowned. "We're not talking about that, Richard. I want you to keep it in mind that Weetoppin's an Indian and different from us. They're savages, these Indians." He stopped. "Besides, that's the way the House of Burgesses wants it."

So that's what this was all about. After church I'd heard them saying that the House of Burgesses had passed a law that said the settlers could have Indians to work for them, but that Indians couldn't live in the settlers' houses. I noticed that Laydon didn't pay any attention to that part of it, and I didn't bring it up. When you got down to it, the Burgesses were saying that us and the Indians were enemies, and we'd better keep that in mind.

Back when we first came over, Powhatan, who was the big chief of most of the Indians around Virginia, figured that maybe he could get the English on his side against his own enemies. With our guns and cannons, Powhatan figured we could help make him an even bigger chief than he already was. So he went easy on the English at first because he figured he could wipe us out any time he wanted: there were thousands of Indians and only a few dozen English, and most of them sick and dying anyway. But now we'd got ourselves built up to over a thousand, with more coming all the time, and it wouldn't be so easy to wipe us out.

The new chief, Opechancanough, seemed like he was going to be tougher with us. So when our new governor came over, he passed the law that Indians weren't to come into Jamestown unless they had a good reason to be there. This new idea, from the House of Burgesses, of not being too friendly with Indians was a part of all that, I reckoned. But it wasn't going to stop me from being friendly with Weetoppin.

Laydon went back up to the house for something. Susan came down the row to where I was working. "I heard all that, Richard," she said.

"About not being friends with Weetoppin?"

"About the Indians being savages and all. They're not so bad. They've got souls like us. The minister will tell you that. He said so in church."

I said, "I guess I wasn't listening," which was most likely true. In church, I was always trying to keep myself awake by dreaming about the grand house and fancy clothes I would have when I got out of my indenture and got rich growing tobacco. "I hate it when he says things about Weetoppin. He won't stab me in the back."

"Don't pay any attention to Laydon," Susan said. "He's not as smart as he thinks he is. You're as smart as he is."

"He was smart enough to get into the House of Burgesses. I don't guess I'm that smart."

"Yes you are," she said. "Someday you'll realize it."

"I don't know when 'someday' is anymore. I don't think it'll ever come."

She smiled and put her arm around my shoulder. "Someday always comes." Then we saw Laydon and Weetoppin coming out of the house, so we went back to work squashing bugs. I was feeling better than I had in a long time.

But I noticed that Laydon was keeping an eye on me and Weetoppin. If we got to fooling around at dinner, making jokes at each other and such, he'd break it up real quick. Once when we were by the water barrel washing up for supper, I accidentally splashed Weetoppin in the face. He turned around and flung half a dipper of water at me. I reached into the barrel with my hand and flipped some water at him. Just then Laydon popped out of the door and grabbed Weetoppin by the shirt front. "You!" he shouted. "Keep your hands to yourself." He let go of

Weetoppin and spun to face me. "Richard, I warned you," he said. Then he went back into the house. Weetoppin stared at Laydon's back, breathing hard. I knew what he was thinking: *Someday I kill him.*

But Laydon couldn't keep an eye on us every minute, for we had too much to do. The tobacco leaves were ripening, and we'd begun to pick them. We had to go around the field every day and pick the ones that were ripe. Pick them too soon and they wouldn't cure right; let them go too long and they'd wither and crumble. We carried the picked leaves up to the tobacco barn, tied them into bunches, and hung them from the beams to dry. The tobacco barn had wide gaps between the boards so the breezes could pass through and help dry the tobacco.

Then the leaves had to be cured with smoke. Oh, it was a devilish amount of work, and we were hard at it from daybreak until it got too dark to see. Blame hot and muggy most of the time, and we were mighty glad of a thunderstorm from time to time to cool things down— although to be honest, I was pretty scared of thunder and lightning. Didn't like that crashing and flashing one bit. I had heard of people being hit by lightning—going along peaceable, thinking about what they were going to have for supper, or thinking about being rich from tobacco when they got through with their indentures . . . then bang! Just like that, they were dead and never knew what hit them. Didn't have a second's warning. I figured I'd want a couple of seconds to get my mind arranged for it, but with lightning you didn't get even a second's warning. You were alive and easy at the beginning of the second and dead before the second had passed. . . . Still, a good storm cooled things down for a while.

One day after dinner Laydon took Weetoppin by the arm and held him. "Weetoppin, I want to talk to you."

Weetoppin looked up at him—his face still as a wall, so Laydon couldn't see what he was thinking. He just stared up with a flat look. But I knew that Weetoppin was mighty suspicious, for it wasn't like Laydon to get into a conversation with him.

Laydon pretended he didn't notice Weetoppin's flat look. He was trying to be friendly. "Weetoppin, this Weyanock village of yours. It's that place about 40 miles up the James River, right?"

Weetoppin waited a bit before he spoke, trying to figure out what Laydon was up to. "Maybe. Maybe 30. Maybe 50." He wasn't going to give anything away that he didn't have to.

Laydon looked a little annoyed but put his friendly face on again. "That's what I figured—about 40. I remember seeing it once 2 or 3 years back when we were up that way trading for corn." He paused. "You reckon they got their corn in by now? It's been a good year for it. They must have a lot laid by."

Weetoppin shrugged. "Don't know."

Another look of annoyance flashed across Laydon's face, but he smoothed it away. "Well, they must have. It's September. They'll have their corn in. The only thing is, they might have hidden it. Those blame Indians have been doing that recent. We need somebody to find out where it is. I figured you might be able to do that, seeing as it's your own people."

The whole thing was making me feel mighty uneasy. Weetoppin would never sell out his own people. I knew that. "Sir, Weetoppin can't go back to his village. You know why."

"Oh, I don't expect him to waltz in there and ask. He can slip in at night and ask his father about it. Maybe some of the other kids'll know. He can make up a story that we ran him off and he's near starved. Just wants a little corn for himself. Somebody's bound to take pity on him and take him out to where the corn is hid."

Why the devil didn't Laydon understand that Weetoppin would never do something like that? He hadn't wanted to run off from his village, he had to for what he'd done. But that didn't mean he would sell them out.

Weetoppin kept his face dead still. "English going to raid Weyanock corn."

"No, no, not raid. Nothing like that. We want to trade. But we need to know if they got anything to trade and where it is, so they can't lie about it. Indians lie about everything."

Weetoppin didn't say anything but went on staring into Laydon's face. I figured he was feeling about as much scorn for Laydon as anyone could feel, but none of it showed. "In village, nobody gonna tell Weetoppin nothing. Kill me first."

"Your father wouldn't kill you. Ask him."

"Father won't tell me nothing about corn."

I saw that Laydon figured Weetoppin was just being stubborn. "Look, Weetoppin," he said, "I know it's a risk for you. It's worth a good knife to me."

Weetoppin turned his head to look out the window at the woods and the sky. I knew him well enough: he was wishing he'd never killed that boy. He was wishing he was back home in his village with his father, his cousins and aunts, and the kids he'd grown up with and couldn't talk to anymore. I knew clear as I knew my own name that he'd give anything to put things back to where they were before. But he couldn't do that. I felt mighty sad for him. Much as I'd miss having him for a friend, I wished he could go home to his village too. There wasn't anything I could do about that either.

"A good, long metal knife with bone handle," he said. He'd decided something, but I didn't know what.

"Good," Laydon said, clapping Weetoppin on the shoulder. "Now we got to work it out about getting you up there. I'll let you know in a couple of days."

Weetoppin didn't say anything. He just took another look beyond the tobacco field to where his village was, somewhere up the James River.

I wanted to know what Weetoppin was planning to do. I knew for certain that he wasn't going to tell Laydon where that corn was hid, even if he could find out—which I wasn't sure he could. He was going to get a good knife out of it anyway. But I decided to let it go for a while. It wasn't any of my business, when you got down

75

to it. If Weetoppin wanted to tell me, he would.

Two days later, Laydon sent Weetoppin over to Henry Spofford's place with a message that he'd written on a piece of paper. I started to go out to the tobacco field, but Laydon called me back. "Richard, I've been talking to some of the other men. They want you to go along with Weetoppin to the Weyanock village."

I was plenty surprised. "What for? I can't speak Algonquian, except about six words." I could speak a little more than that, for I'd learned some from Weetoppin, but not much.

"They don't trust Weetoppin. He might just hide out in the woods for a couple of days and then tell us that the Weyanocks didn't have any corn left—that they'd traded it off to another tribe or something. They want you to go along and see for yourself where the corn is hidden."

It was the most awful pinch to put me in. On one side of it, I was English and bound to be loyal to my own people, just like Weetoppin was to his. You could say all you wanted about the English coming to Virginia, where they weren't wanted, and pushing the Indians back so they'd have land for farms and such. But as far as that went, the Indians weren't any more kind and generous to each other than we were to them. Powhatan, he fought all the other tribes around and took them over when he could. He made the other tribes bring him mountains of corn every year. And deerskins, meat, beads—whatever he wanted from them. It didn't seem to me that the English were treating the Indians much worse than the Indians treated each other.

The plain truth is, I was mighty proud of being English. We had it all over the Indians. We had books and writing and ciphering numbers. We had great ships and compasses and all kinds of metal things. We had clocks and snug houses, and I didn't know what all else. Not that I had any clocks or compasses of my own. And I couldn't write or cipher numbers any better than Weetoppin could, as far as that went. But still, I figured we were better than the Indians, and I was proud of it. Of course, Weetoppin, he didn't see it that way. He figured the Indians were better than we were. It didn't make sense to me, but that was the way he thought.

The truth was, I just *felt* English. I was glad I was English and not an Indian. But even so, I wasn't going to sell out Weetoppin. I just couldn't. I had to get out of going to the Weyanock village. "Sir, how am I going to go to an Indian village?"

"I don't know. We haven't figured that out yet. Maybe we'll disguise you as an Indian."

"Sir, I don't look anything like an Indian."

"Well, I don't know. We'll figure something out."

I took a deep breath. "I don't want to do it," I said.

Laydon frowned. He wasn't used to me disobeying his orders. "What do you mean you don't want to do it? I knew you were getting too friendly with Weetoppin."

"It isn't that, sir. If they catch me, they'll torture me to death."

"Oh, they won't catch you. You just have to be careful.

77

Weetoppin knows the lay of the land out there. You'll be safe enough with him."

"Still, I don't want to do it." I was taking a big risk on getting smacked. "Why doesn't one of the men go with him?" The whole thing was making me mad.

"You're his friend. He'll trust you more. He wouldn't trust any of the men."

That was the whole point of the thing: Weetoppin would trust me, and I wasn't about to go back on him. I was losing my temper. "I'm not going to do it."

"Well, you *are* going to do it, Richard. I'm telling you so. You don't have any choice. If it's a risk, it's a risk. A lot of men have got themselves killed out here doing things they didn't want to do."

"I'm not going to do it!" I knew he was going to hit me sooner or later but I didn't care, for I was mad. "I'm just a piece of trash to you. I don't mean anything more to you than one of the chickens that gets butchered on Sunday. You don't care if I go out there and get tortured, so long as you get some use out of me."

"Oh no, you're wrong about that, Richard," he said. "You're valuable to me. You're a good worker. I wouldn't want to risk you. I said so to the other men, and they said that if anything happened to you they'd get the Burgesses to pay me for you."

"That's just what I mean!" I blazed out. "You're about as much a Christian as that pig we got running around—"

He swung his hand around and smacked me as hard as he could across the face. Even though I knew it was coming, it was too powerful for me, and it knocked me over backwards. I fell over on my bottom and sat there, shaking my head to clear the dizziness. He jumped forward until he was straddling me, bent over, grabbed me by the shirt, and pulled me up toward him. Then he whacked me across the face, not so hard this time but aiming deliberate for my nose. I felt something begin to run down across my lips. I licked and tasted blood.

"Richard, I told you what you're going to do, and you're going to do it." He strode out of the house. I got up and wiped my nose on my sleeve. Then I went out to the water barrel and dipped my whole face into it. The coolness of it made me feel better.

Right then, I think I would have been able to kill him if anyone had suggested it.

Chapter 8

We spent the afternoon in the tobacco shed, bundling leaves. The sweet smell of tobacco was in the air. It was the beginning of September, plenty hot and humid, and we were dripping with sweat the whole time. The bundles of leaves hanging down from the rafters cut into what little breeze there was, so whenever we figured Laydon couldn't see us we ducked out of the shed, raced up to the water barrel, and poured a dipper of water over ourselves. The water in the barrel was warmish, but even so it cooled us down. I'd have given anything for a chance to go swimming, but there was no hope of that.

My nose was swollen and clogged, and I had to breathe through my mouth. When I talked, the words sounded funny. But I could talk well enough to tell Weetoppin what had happened. "They want me to go with you. The men do. They want me to see to it that you really find out where the corn is hid."

He looked at me. "What you say?"

"I said I wouldn't do it. That's why he smacked me."

"Does it hurt much?"

"Not as bad as a whipping, but bad enough."

He looked away from me and then back out of the corner of his eye. "You gonna go with me?"

"I have to. He's like to kill me if I don't." I gave him a steady look and took a deep breath through my mouth. "You were planning on lying about it, weren't you?"

He gave me his defiant look. "Sure. Wouldn't you, if you was me?"

"Where does that leave me, Weetoppin?"

We stared at each other. We were both trapped. "Maybe you can be too sick to go."

"That won't mean anything to him. Believe me, I don't want to go out there and take a chance on getting tortured to death. But he's going to keep knocking me around until I do it. You know how he gets when you contradict him. He won't rest until he gets you to do what he says."

"Maybe we should run away," he said.

"I've thought about that every day for six years. I never can figure out where to run to."

"The Indians. Lots of English run off to the Indians."

"The old governor, he tortured a couple of men for doing it."

"Still, there's English out in them villages."

"Weetoppin, you can't go back to the Indians yourself."

"Maybe we find some Indians outside of Powhatan. Up the bay somewhere. No more whippin'. You be free of Laydon."

I thought about it. Could I really run off and join some Indian village? Live like an Indian? Learn how to hunt and fish with them, do their holy dances and sing their holy songs instead of going to church? Live in a little

Indian hut instead of a house, eat out of a clay pot with my fingers instead of out of a trencher? It would take a mighty lot of getting used to, I figured. I'd never shot a bow in my life. I wasn't trained to do such things. "I'm not an Indian, Weetoppin. Nothing against the Indians, but I was raised to English ways, and they suit me."

"Then you got to lie about corn too."

"I can't do it. What if we run out of corn come spring and people starve to death? It'd be because of me. Because I wouldn't tell where the Indians' corn was."

"That our corn. What right English have to take it?"

He had me there. I thought for a minute, trying to come up with something, but I couldn't. "None, I guess. Still, what if they found out I'd lied about it?"

"Laydon said the English didn't have starving time no more. Have plenty of corn."

I thought about that too. It was true. We were supposed to have plenty of corn. "I'll ask Laydon," I said. "Maybe they'll decide not to do it."

There wasn't much hope of that, but when I had a chance I brought it up with Laydon. "What do we need Indian corn for?" I said. "I thought we had plenty ourselves."

"Oh, we do," he said. "But the governor doesn't want to risk it. He says there's no telling how many new people will come in over the winter. Best be prepared."

"What if me and Weetoppin go out there and can't find the corn?"

"You better find it, Richard. I'm warning you. I told

you not to get too friendly with Weetoppin. Whose side are you on?"

I knew I'd better answer that real quick. "I'm not going over to the Indians, sir. I wouldn't do that. But maybe we really won't be able to find the corn."

"Just find it," he said. And that was the end of that.

I could see that Laydon was trying to make himself important among the settlers. He had an advantage, for he lived just over the river from Jamestown, where the governor lived and where the House of Burgesses was supposed to meet each year. Most of the settlers were spread up the James for miles and couldn't get into Jamestown easy. But Laydon only had to row across the river in a skiff. I was pretty sure this whole corn thing was his idea in the first place, because of having a Weyanock working for him. He was going to push it through and get the others to talking about how smart he was, knew how to handle the Indians and such. I figured about half the reason for this whole scheme wasn't so much for the corn, but to get other settlers to admiring Laydon. But of course, I couldn't say that to him.

While Laydon and his men were making their plans, something happened that took our minds off it. A Dutch sea captain brought in a load of 20 Negroes for sale.

Most of us English had never seen a black person before. Heard about them but had never seen them. It was all the talk after church. A few people who'd been down to the islands in the Caribbean had seen Negroes working in the sugarcane fields there. "They can stand the heat the way a white person can't," one of them said. "It's natural because they was raised in Africa where it's blame hot, and they got used to it."

Still, people were of two minds about the Negroes. Some said they didn't like them and didn't want any around. "I seen them down there on the islands. More like animals than human beings, if you ask me. I think we could do without them in Virginia."

"Oh, I wouldn't agree with that," another one said. "I worked with one of those Negroes on a Portuguese ship I was on once. Seemed a good enough sort. Might make good servants if they can stand the heat like they say."

I was mighty curious to see one. Then we heard that Henry Spofford had got one. "What do you suppose he's like, Weetoppin?" I asked. We were in the tobacco shed, bundling leaves and hanging them from the rafters. "I'd give a lot to see him."

"You certain there are black people?"

"Oh, plenty of them. They come from Africa. Over there, everybody's black. It's from the sun."

He wasn't sure he believed it. "Sound blame strange," he said. "Where's Africa?"

"I'm not exactly sure," I said. "A good long way from here, I reckon."

"Near England?"

"Oh no, a good long way from there too, I reckon. It's awful hot there."

"They're really black, Richard?"

"Maybe we can figure out a way to go over to Spofford's plantation and take a look."

But we couldn't because Laydon and his men had got their plan ready. I was to be disguised as an Indian. I would wear a loincloth and have my hair braided over to one side like Weetoppin's. I didn't have as much hair as he did, but I had enough for a short braid. I didn't like any of it very much. For one thing, I wasn't used to running around naked, with just a loincloth to cover me. We English didn't go around with our legs bare, but wore pants and stockings and such. Of course, Weetoppin had been wearing English clothes since he'd come to live with us. But before that, he'd gone around naked as a jay until he was around 10, so he was used to it. I wasn't. I didn't like showing so much of myself off.

But the men figured it was safer, and I guess it was. I wouldn't fool anyone up close, but at a distance we'd look like a couple of Indian boys hunting for turtles or snakes or such. We were each to carry a knife, and wear a couple bags of cornbread and pork tied around our waists.

To tell the truth, I wouldn't have minded the whole thing so much if it hadn't been for lying about the corn. It was going to be an adventure—a mighty scary adventure, that was true, for it wasn't any joke about getting our heads smashed in with clubs if some Indians caught us spying. Still, it was a good deal more exciting than picking tobacco, although we'd just about got the picking done, which was why they'd set it for this time. So if it hadn't been for lying about the corn, I'd have been looking forward to it—scared, oh yes, but game for it.

The lying bothered me a good deal. Whatever I did

was going to be wrong. It'd be wrong if we found the corn and wrong if we didn't; wrong if I told about it and wrong if I didn't. There wasn't any answer to it, and that bothered me a lot.

Susan rigged up a loincloth for me and braided my hair. I felt mighty embarrassed about the whole thing and felt even worse when Henry Spofford came riding up the road and turned into our place when Susan was doing the braiding. I had hauled a bench out into the yard for more light and was sitting there in my loincloth while Susan fooled with my hair. When Spofford pulled in, I started to stand up.

"Go on with what you're doing," he said. "I was just curious to see what kind of Indian the boy would make. It didn't seem like such a good idea to me." He wasn't looking at me, but at Susan. "Pretty neat job, Susan. I'd dress like an Indian myself if I thought you'd do my braid."

Susan blushed and giggled. It wasn't like her to blush and giggle. She was usually the serious sort. "I don't think you'd make much of an Indian, sir."

"Why Susan, you're wrong there. I'd make a superb Indian." He'd hardly given me a look. "Now you're the one who couldn't pass for an Indian, Susan. Not with your golden hair and rosy English cheeks." Finally, he looked at me. "That boy is mighty lucky to have you for a hairdresser. What's your name, son? Richard, did they say?"

"Richard Ayre, sir."

"From Ayreshire?"

"I don't rightly know, sir. I don't know who my father and mother were. People always called me Richard Ayre is all I know."

"London orphan, then."

"Yes, sir."

"Well, you don't look much like an Indian, Richard. I hope Laydon knows what he's doing."

"They reckon I'll look like an Indian from a distance."

"Better keep your distance," he said. Then he went back to Susan. "Come over for a visit sometime if Laydon can spare you." He touched the horse with his whip and off he went. Susan went back to braiding my hair.

"He didn't take any interest in me at all," I said. "I'm the one who's likely to be killed."

"I don't think killing was on his mind," she said.

I tried to turn my head around to look at her, but she had a hold of my braid and wouldn't let me. "What do you mean by that?"

"Sit still and stop squirming, Richard. How can I do your braid when you keep jiggling around like that?"

We set off the next day in the skiff—Laydon, me and Weetoppin, and two other men with muskets. The skiff was pretty full, but we had a good breeze from the northeast and didn't need the oars. Me and Weetoppin lay in the bottom of the boat so as not to be spotted by any Indians along the way. Indian villages were most usually set up along the river or just a little back from it. We didn't want them noticing a couple boys aboard the skiff on the way up the river but none on the way back down.

The northeast breeze meant that there was likely to be a storm. I wasn't so sure I wanted to be out in the woods with thunder and lightning cracking and rain pouring down. I lay there on the bottom of the boat looking up at the sky, feeling funny in my braid and loincloth, hoping that the rain would hold off. Maybe we could find a shelter in the woods. Sometimes you came up on an abandoned Indian hut.

Taken altogether, I was feeling mighty strange. It was funny thinking that in a day or so I might be dead out there in some Indian village, my head bashed in or my bones all broken. I reached up to touch my face, my hand moving around to feel the bones under my skin—my cheekbones, my forehead, my skull. Now they were all solid and alive. In a couple days they might all be trash, like the broken bones and pieces of meat in the pit behind our house.

We'd got about two miles upriver when one of the men suddenly said, "I thought I saw something move in the woods over on the north bank."

Weetoppin sat up and looked around. "Deer," he said.

Laydon quickly put his hand on Weetoppin's head and pushed him back down. "Keep your head down," he said.

The man who'd seen the movement looked down at Weetoppin. "You sure it was a deer? Didn't seem so to me."

"Deer," Weetoppin said. "I saw it plain."

"He's probably right," the other man said. "These Indians got good eyesight."

With the good wind, we were making lively time up the river. I was getting mighty restless lying there on the bottom of the skiff, not able to move my head or anything. Still, it was a good deal more comfortable being with those muskets than it was going to be once we got out. There wasn't anything I could do about it one way or another, so I lay there staring at the sky and thinking of what kind of house I'd have when I owned 100 acres of tobacco fields and was rich.

We'd been gone about two hours now. We were about halfway to where me and Weetoppin were to get out when one of the men spotted two Indians on the south bank of the river. "Look," he said, pointing. "Indians."

Immediately Weetoppin sat up. "Where?" he said. He'd hardly got the word started when Laydon grabbed him by the hair and jerked him back down. "I told you to keep your blame head down, Weetoppin. One more time and I'll whack you good."

"Anyone know who they might be?" asked one of the men.

"There's a Quiyoughcohannock village around here somewhere," the other man said.

"You know about that, Weetoppin?" Laydon asked.

Weetoppin started to raise his head again but thought better of it. "Quiyoughcohannock village on south side, Paspahegh on north."

"Might be either," Laydon said. "They friendly with the Weyanocks?"

"Sometimes," Weetoppin said. "Sometimes make war."

89

It worried me. "Will they track us, Weetoppin?"

"Maybe," he said. That wasn't much comfort. You never could get a straight answer out of Weetoppin when he didn't want to give you one.

"Can they keep up with us?" I asked.

"You boys hush up," Laydon commanded.

I went back to staring at the clouds. They were a little thicker now and gliding up the river with us. Then Laydon said to the helmsman, "Ease off. See that marsh there, in that cove? Push in just ahead of that, where the trees hang over the banks. We can slip the boys over the side there. The trees'll cover them."

I looked at Weetoppin. He was staring up at the clouds, nothing on his face. But I was sure there was a lot going on in his mind.

The skiff headed toward the bank. I went on staring at the sky. Suddenly the leafy branch of a tree appeared overhead so close I could touch it. Right after it came another, and another. The boat bumped lightly on the bank. The men grabbed hold of the branches and pulled them lower to screen us off from the riverside. Laydon climbed out of the boat and onto the bank. "All right," he said. "You boys slide over the side. Don't stand up, just slip out." We did it and then crawled back about 20 feet into the woods, where we'd be hid from view from the water. Then we stood up. I was mighty glad of it, for we'd been lying in the bottom of that blame skiff for four hours, as close as I could figure from the sun.

Laydon looked us over for a minute. "I don't reckon

any Indians saw you get out. Got your food bags? We'll be back in three days to pick you up. Soon as you figure out where the corn is, come back here and hole up." Then he got back into the skiff and pushed off from the bank. They back-watered out into the river and began to row downstream against the wind. We watched the skiff get smaller and smaller until it disappeared around a bend.

Chapter 9

We went back into the woods a ways and sat down in the shadows, our backs against tree trunks. I looked at Weetoppin. What did he have in mind to do? I wasn't going to ask straight out, for that might lead to an argument. And it wouldn't do for us to argue right then. "Do you think any Indians know we're here? Do you think they spotted us coming up the river?"

"They know we here."

A chill went over me. "You sure?"

"I sure. Why you think I sit up in skiff? That wasn't no deer I saw."

I stared at him. "You did it on purpose?"

"Sure."

"But why? You'll bring Indians down on us for certain."

"If Indians come, we got good reason not to hunt corn. Then you don't gotta lie."

I sat there looking at him. It was mighty smart. If some Indians came after us when we'd hardly got out of the skiff, we'd have to run for it. There wouldn't be any chance of looking around for corn, and it wouldn't be on my head if Jamestown ran short of food in the spring.

"Weetoppin, that was real smart. But what if these Indians catch us?"

He shrugged. "We die. Indian not afraid to die."

It was true. They had a different feeling about it. Most of us English would do pretty much anything to get out of dying. The Indians would rather die than beg and plead. "Don't you mind getting your brains smashed?"

He shrugged. "Not afraid."

"Yes, but wouldn't you mind? I sure would."

He started to say something but I never found out what it was, for there came a low sound from the river, a sort of bump. If we hadn't been thinking about Indians, we mightn't have paid it any attention, for it was only a small noise. But it was enough. I put my finger to my lips, but Weetoppin was already on his feet, moving quiet as a shadow through the trees deeper into the woods. Then I was moving after him, my heart racing, trying to put my feet down as soft as I could and slip through the branches so they wouldn't slap around. Those Indians would know we'd been sent to spy on them and nobody ever did but one thing to spies, no matter what side they were on.

Now behind us I could hear soft noises. They'd come after us in a canoe, I figured, and were climbing up onto the bank. How many were there? Those Indian canoes could hold a good many people. There could be four or five of them, but it didn't matter. One Indian with a bow could shoot us both down in half a minute.

Weetoppin was now a good 20 feet ahead of me. He

was trained to slip through the woods quiet to stalk animals, and I wasn't. I felt scared and sore at myself for being so clumsy. I struggled on, trying to put my feet down softly. Then Weetoppin stopped and I caught up to him.

We stood behind the trunk of a big oak, out of sight from the direction of the river. The sky above was real gray. It was going to storm soon. I whispered, "Are they Weyanocks?"

"I reckon. Weyanock village not far."

"Will they be able to track us in the woods?"

"Maybe. They catch us pretty quick if they do. They look for leaves turned over and marks in dirt."

"What if we circle back to the river and swim over to the other side?"

"Risky. Maybe left somebody to guard canoe. Won't leave canoe alone for us to take."

"We could go down river a ways until we're around a bend from the canoe."

"Maybe."

My heart was still racing, my muscles tight, my stomach cold. "One way or another we got to get moving."

"We try it," he said. Somewhere back by the river we could hear faint voices—a little sound, then silence, then another sound, and more silence. We started off through the woods until we'd gone 100 yards deeper into them. I figured we were near a quarter-mile back from the river. Far enough so nobody on the river would hear us moving, if we were quiet about it. Then we turned east to run parallel to the river, going downstream. I was still having trouble keeping up with Weetoppin—it was amazing to me how fast and quiet he could move in the woods. They were home to him, just as comfortable as the house and tobacco fields were to me. I resolved that when I had a chance, I'd get him to teach me how to go through the woods like that. If we lived long enough.

We were going along like that when I saw ahead a little trail in the woods, winding south away from the river. It wasn't much of a trail, only a dirt track a few inches wide. Deer trail, I thought. Plenty of deer in these woods. Then I saw something laying on the ground alongside the trail—an ear of corn. Someone or something had eaten most of the kernels off of it—deer or raccoon most likely. Raccoon could have snatched it out of a Weyanock field and carried it out here to eat. A little farther up the trail there was another ear of corn. It was a good excuse to stop running and catch my breath. I stared on up the trail. Laying in the woods a couple yards from the trail was an Indian basket, woven of reeds.

It wasn't a deer trail after all. I leaned forward and peered up the trail. Up there was a shape, just a shape, in the woods amongst the leaves and branches. But I knew what that shape was, all right. It was the hut where the Weyanocks stored their corn. There wasn't any doubt about it—the corn that had got chewed and dropped along the way by animals, the reed basket that had got lost. No doubt about it all. I wanted in the worst way to go on up that little trail to see for sure, but I couldn't.

Not with the Weyanocks coming along behind us. I took a deep breath and set myself in motion again.

Weetoppin was standing in the woods 50 feet from me, waiting. "Got to keep moving, Richard," he said.

"I know," I said. Behind us there were faint sounds. We set off again, this time heading back to the river. On and on we went, and then ahead I could see the woods become brighter. The river was coming up to us. We kept going. When we could see the water through the trees, we bent low and slipped forward easy, until we were six feet from the bank. We dropped to the leaves and slid to the edge of the water. There were some willow trees with yellow leaves leaning out over the river. The branches drooped down until they were touching the water. They cut down on our vision. We held still and listened. Behind us we heard noises. "Let's go," I said. We slipped into the river, trying to swim without splashing, and paddled out to where the willow branches hit the water. We stuck our heads through the branches.

We could see a good distance down river. Nothing in sight. Upriver the stream bent away from us, and we couldn't see along the bank for more than 100 feet. "Weetoppin, you think there's a canoe around the bend?"

"Maybe," he said.

"We got to chance it," I said. I looked directly across the river. It wasn't more than half a mile across. I could swim that easy, even with the current. "We should swim across. By the time they figure out where we are, we'll be a good piece away." Weetoppin nodded. We didn't have much choice. Then from above came the distant thumping of thunder. "Thunderstorm," I said. "Let's get across before it hits."

We slipped through the willow branches and into the open river. About four strokes out, I turned to look back toward the shore. A good ways back into the woods, something was moving. I turned back and dug into the water. Being as it was September, the water was low and the current not too strong. We tried to keep our heads low in the water in case somebody was looking out at us through the trees. Then, when we were about halfway across, came the rumble of thunder, like somebody was moving barrels around. Last thing I wanted was to get caught in the water during a thunderstorm. If lightning struck anywhere near, it'd kill us for sure. I began to swim faster. I hadn't gone more than five strokes when the rain hit sudden, streaming down onto the river and bouncing around. There came a great flash of lightning and then a blast of thunder that went rolling down the sky. Then another flash of lightning brightened things so much that the woods across seemed to jump out at us and then jump back when the light went off. I drove my arms into the water as hard as I could, desperate to get onto dry land. On and on we went, the thunder rolling and the lightning flashing and the woods jumping out at us.

We closed in on the bank. Suddenly Weetoppin shouted, "Richard, hold up!" But I wasn't going to hold up. Whatever it was could wait until I hit dry land. I made the bank and clambered up, skidding and sliding,

and heaved myself into the woods. For a minute, I lay
there panting and shivering in the rain. Finally I sat up
and looked around for Weetoppin. Just at that moment
the lightning struck again. There was no sign of
Weetoppin—not in the water, not scrambling up the
bank toward me. I turned around to look into the woods,
thinking he might have got ahead of me somehow. The
lightning struck once more, and out of the trees popped
about six of the biggest Indians I ever saw. That was why
Weetoppin had hollered for me to hold up. I jumped to
my feet and made a dash for the riverbank, but they were
out of the woods and on me just as I hit the bank. They
grabbed me and shoved me hard onto the wet ground,
making my head ring. Then I was being marched along a
trail through the woods, surrounded by Indians.

Oh, I felt awful. Soaking wet and shivering, tired from
that hard swim, and plenty scared for certain. Just being
so close to those big Indians wearing nothing but
loincloths and moccasins, their bare skin slick with water,
was scary. Why hadn't I held up when Weetoppin
shouted? What the devil was the matter with me? Why
hadn't I any sense?

Where was Weetoppin? Turned around and swum
back out into the river. Gone upstream or down, looking
for a place to hide. The Indians must have known there
were two of us in the water. That thick rain made it hard
to see very far into the river, except when the lightning
came. Then you could see every ripple of it. Could they
have shot him? Maybe he was drifting down the river
toward Jamestown with an arrow sticking out of his back.

I shuddered and tried not to think of that.

We went along the trail through the woods for about five minutes. Then the woods opened out into a cornfield. The corn was all picked now, but the melons and squash were still growing on their vines. The Indians always planted melons, squash, and beans amongst the corn. The bean vines would climb the cornstalks as the corn grew, and the big leaves of the squash and melons covered the earth to keep the weeds down and the moisture in. It was a clever thing, but even so you could grow more food the English way if you weren't set on using every square inch for tobacco.

Beyond the cornfield was the village. Paspahegh, I reckoned. Scared as I was, and shivering, I was still curious. I'd never seen an Indian village close up—seen them from the river a few times when I'd gone up the James with Laydon, but never seen one up close. Their lodges were scattered around here and there, maybe 20 of them. To make them, the Indians dug poles into the ground and pulled the tops together to make a frame. They covered the frame with skins or woven reed mats.

The Indians were mostly inside because of the storm— but as we marched past, a head would stick out here and there to have a look at me. Not that an English person was strange to them, for we'd been in Virginia for 12 years now and had mingled with them a good deal. But they didn't see English in their own village too often.

We went on to what I judged was the center of the village. There was a bigger house. One of the Indians guarding me pulled aside the deerskin hanging over the door and pointed. I ducked and went in.

It was mighty dark in there. The Indians didn't have lamps or candles. The only light came from a little fire in a circle of stones in the center of the house. Along the walls were low log bunks heaped with blankets. A woman was crouched by the fire, stirring something in a pot. Three Indian men sat on the bunks. I felt like their eyes were gazing right through me. I wished I could shrink down to nothing and disappear.

Then as my eyes got used to the light, I saw that one of the Indians wasn't an Indian at all. He was an Englishman. He wore a loincloth and moccasins and had a deerskin flung over his shoulders, but he was English all right. He had blond hair, blue eyes, and a good deal of hair on his chest, which Indians didn't usually have. I was curious as could be to know how he'd got there, but I had sense enough not to ask.

I was mighty glad to see him. Not that he was likely to do me any favors, for he'd gone over to the Indians and was bound to take their side. Still, it was comforting to have somebody around who could speak my language and would have some idea of how I felt.

Now one of the other Indians turned to him and said something to him in Algonquian. The Englishman nodded. Then he said, "What the devil are you doing, wandering around the woods in a loincloth? Whose idea was that?"

I had to be mighty careful. I didn't mind getting Laydon and them in trouble, for it was their fault that I was out there in a loincloth. I hadn't wanted to come, that was certain. But I blame well didn't want him to get the idea I was spying for corn. "I was supposed to look like an Indian," I said.

"I could have figured that out for myself," he said. "You didn't fool anybody for six minutes. Every Indian up and down the river knew you was English." The other Indians sat quiet, listening, although I don't know how much they understood.

"How'd they know so fast?" I was stalling, hoping I could think up a good reason for why I was running around in a loincloth.

"Anyone who seen you from half a mile away would know you wasn't any Indian. You look no more like an Indian than a frog. The Indians up and down both sides of the river been watching you since you was a mile out of Jamestown. You still haven't answered my question: What was the idea of the loincloth?"

"We were supposed to find out if anyone had any corn to trade. They figured that if I was wearing a loincloth, the Indians wouldn't run away from us." That seemed like a pretty smart explanation to me.

It wasn't. "They wasn't likely to run away from two *boys*, was they?"

I blushed. I didn't much like being stupid. "I guess they didn't think of that." It was pretty limp and I went on blushing.

"Who was supposed to have this corn?" he asked.

"The Weyanocks. Mr. Laydon—my master—heard

101

they might have extra this year."

"Laydon? I know him. Handy with a whip, as I recall."

"He likes whipping boys. He doesn't need much of an excuse."

"I feel sorry for you. That's why I run off. My master had a lot of experience with a whip and knew how to cut skin. He liked to draw blood. Three years into my indenture I knew I'd never last out four more. Either he'd kill me or I'd kill him. So I left. Didn't bother to say goodbye."

I was mighty curious. "Do you like being an Indian? Don't you miss being with English people?" I wondered if the Indians understood what I was saying.

"Oh, I might go back if there was a reason for it. If I could get out of my indenture and set up in business for myself getting rich off tobacco. But this suits me pretty well. I got an Indian wife, a couple children. They'd find living in a house and wearing shoes and going to church a little hard to get used to." He turned and said something to the Indians sitting on the log bunks. They nodded and he turned back to me. "Now, your story don't quite hang together. Why'd they send out a boy in a loincloth to ask about trading corn? Why not go out with muskets and ask for it themselves."

I was stumped for a reason. All I could think of to say was, "I don't know." I blushed again.

"Oh, don't give me that. You know blame well you was spying."

I was cornered and I figured I'd better tell the truth. Some of it, anyway. I was mighty worried about being tortured. Maybe he'd feel sorry for me if I was being honest. "Well, that's true." I said. "We were supposed to spy to see if the Weyanocks had extra corn to trade. But they caught us as soon as we got out of the boat. We jumped in the river to get away. Just then the storm hit, and they didn't bother to follow us. I guess they didn't want to get caught in the water with lightning flashing around."

Once again he stopped to say something to the Indians on the bunks, and then he turned back to me. "You wasn't sent out to spy for corn in general, was you? See what the Weyanocks had, then cross over and see what the Paspaheghs had to offer?"

"No, no, we weren't to have anything to do with the Paspaheghs. I promise." My stories weren't coming off so good and I was beginning to feel cold and sweaty. "The whole thing had to do with the Weyanocks because that was where the Indian boy was from. Laydon and them figured he could slip into their village on the sly and ask somebody where the corn was hid."

The English Indian thought about that for a minute. "That makes sense. But why would an Indian want to go back on his own people? What was he doing with Laydon anyway?"

Most all of it had come out. I didn't see where it would hurt Weetoppin if I told the rest. "He killed a boy in his village and ran away to the English. I caught him

103

stealing a hoe and he hired on with Laydon."

He nodded. "I heard something about that murder. So he was going to spy on his own people?"

It seemed like anything I said was bound to get somebody in trouble. "No, no, he said he wouldn't do it. We were just going to sit around out there in the woods for a couple of days and then go home and say we couldn't find out anything about the corn."

"That makes sense too. But it would make more sense if you decided to see if the Paspaheghs had any corn hid, so you wouldn't go home empty-handed."

"No, no, it wasn't like that at all." I was sweating mighty hard and feeling cold and alone. Suddenly, a thought came to me. "Besides, we weren't going home empty-handed. I know where the Weyanocks hid their corn."

Chapter 10

He stared at me. "Well," he said. "That was a long time coming out, wasn't it?"

I didn't say anything. I figured it was time I kept my mouth shut. He turned his head and said something to the Indians on the bunks. Then he came back to me. "They don't believe you."

"It's true. I saw the place myself." I hoped I had. What if it turned out that the shape I'd seen through the trees was a big rock or an abandoned hut? I tried to wipe some of the sweat off my face with my arm, but my arm was still wet from the rain.

He said something to the Indians and they talked for a while. Then he said to me, "You can show us where this corn is?"

"Yes," I said. "I can take you right there." I had gotten myself into a real bad place now. Suppose it was an abandoned hut and the Weyanocks had dropped the corn and the reed basket when they were moving out? I decided not to think of that. It just had to be a corn hut—that was all there was to it.

The Englishman and the Indians talked among themselves for awhile. I crept in close to the warmth, where the Indian woman was stirring the clay pot. The heat from the fire felt mighty good on my skin, and so did the smell of whatever was cooking in the pot. Deer, I figured, along with the squash and beans. In the fall when the crops were in, the Indians ate mighty good.

The men went on talking for some time. After a while, one of them lifted the skin door and went out. I kept shifting myself around in front of the fire so as to cook myself all over like a piece of meat. The rain was beginning to let up, and there was some hope that I could stay dry if I had to go outside again. I kept thinking about Weetoppin. Was he out in the woods, soaking wet and shivering? Had he headed back for Jamestown? Was he floating down the river with an arrow in his back? I wish we hadn't got split up. I wish I hadn't been so scared of getting struck by lightning in the water and had held up when Weetoppin said to.

After a while, the Indian who'd left came back and chatted with the others some more. Then the Englishman said to me, "What's your name?"

"Richard."

"Richard what?"

"Richard Ayre."

"Your family from Ayreshire back home?"

I shrugged. "Don't know. I was running loose in the streets before I came over. I don't have any family that I know of."

He nodded. "They was always collecting orphans off the streets of London and shipping them to Virginia. They wasn't any more use here than they was back home. Most of 'em died, anyway. You're mighty lucky to be alive.

Of course, you might not be tomorrow. Depends on how
this corn works out. We're gonna take you back across, so
you can show us that store of corn."

I looked at him. "What'll happen if I can't find it?"

"I wouldn't want to be in your shoes if you don't."

"Will they let me go home if I find it?"

"I ain't sure about that. If it was me, I would. But it
ain't gonna be up to me." He said something to the
Indian woman. She got a bowl from a stack by the fire,
filled it with stuff from the pot, and handed it to me. I
dug in, eating with my fingers the way Indians did. It was
mighty good, too—meat, some corn, beans, and other
stuff I couldn't recognize mixed in. First good meal I'd
had in a while, and I was ready for it.

"Let's go," the Englishman said. I stood, and we went
out through the deer hide tent flap. It had quit raining.
The clouds overhead were sailing along pretty good. It
would clear off soon. I took a deep breath. Now all I had
to do was find that corn.

The village was set back from the river a couple
hundred feet. We set off for it in single file, one Indian in
front, then the Englishman, then me, and then another
Indian. The Indians were carrying baskets, hatchets, bows
and arrows. Some Indians had come out of their houses
to see us go by. We reached the riverbank, where there
were some canoes tied up. "All right, Richard Ayre," the
Englishman said, "Where are we going?"

I was desperate to get out of it. "Aren't you afraid that
the Weyanocks will spot us going over?"

"You leave that to us. Where are we going?"

"Head directly across from where I came out of the water upstream. Back in the woods a ways, there's a little trail going south away from the river. The corn hut is up that trail." There was an awful lot of woods across the river.

The Indians piled the baskets into one of the canoes, and we climbed in, with me in the middle and one Indian at the bow and one at the stern, paddling. We headed upriver to where I'd swum across. I didn't know it was the place, for the riverbank all looked the same to me. But they knew—it was as familiar to them as the streets of Jamestown were to me. The Englishman pointed across. "That's it, over there somewhere?"

"As near as I can figure," I said. "It might take me a little while to find it. We had the Weyanocks behind us when we were coming through the woods and I wasn't making notes of things too particular."

He gave me a look. "You sure this corn of yours is real? It ain't a dream you had when you was snoozing last night?"

"No, no," I said. "I'm sure." But I wasn't.

He said something to the Indians. They dug in their paddles and we shot across the river almost as fast as a man could run. Those Indians could make a canoe just fly. Five minutes later we were on the opposite bank. They tucked the canoe in under the willow branches and tied it to a tree. We climbed out. "All right, Richard Ayre, lead on."

I took a deep breath. "What if the Weyanocks come?"

"Never mind that," he said.

I pointed off through the woods. "I think it's that way." I took another deep breath and we started off through the woods. My heart was beating something fierce, and I was sweating. The sky was clearing and the air was getting warm and muggy. It would be real hot soon.

Where was that trail? As best I could remember, we'd come straight toward the river after I'd spotted that trail, and then we'd swum straight across the river. So if I walked straight back from the river, I was bound to hit it. I led them into the woods, going as quick as I could for 50 yards, and then 100 yards, and another 50. After that I stopped. I'd gone too far and missed it.

I stopped and looked at the Englishman. "It's got to be right around here somewhere."

"You sure you didn't dream this whole thing, Richard Ayre?"

"No, no, I swear. I saw it." I looked around, feeling desperate, peering through the woods in every direction. No sight of it. No sight of a path, nor a hump of a hut like a shadow in the woods. No sight of anything. "Let's go back to the river and try again. Maybe I veered off to one side."

We got back to the river, and I turned around and looked into the woods. I was hoping I'd see something that looked familiar. But there was nothing. The woods all seemed the same no matter where I looked. But the path and the hut had to be either to the right or the left of the route I'd just taken. I swallowed and made a guess. "Maybe it was a little more off to the left," I said, pointing. "I think that was it."

"Better be right this time. These Indians don't look none too happy with all this fooling around out here."

"Blame it, it's hard to remember. We were mighty fussed when we ran out of here."

"You'll be mighty fussed if you don't find that corn hut, that's certain."

I was plenty scared. I set off in the new direction, more at an angle to the left. On it went, and on, and on. And then I knew this wasn't any good. I stopped. "This isn't it, either."

The Englishman stood there with his arms folded across his chest like an Indian, looking at me. "Well, I'd say you got about one more chance, Richard Ayre. Try to think back. You say you came straight out of the woods toward the river from where you say the corn hut was."

"As good as I can remember, yes. We weren't doing any zigzags. We wanted to shoot straight for the river and get across."

"And you swam straight across."

"Straight as an arrow. With that lightning and thunder banging and crashing, I was going for the bank as fast as I could. The current isn't too bad this time of year, and—" I stopped. "The current. That's it. All the while we were swimming, the current was carrying us downstream."

"Why of course it was, you idiot. What'd you think it was doing, taking you upstream?"

"That's the problem, then. We'd have hit the opposite bank a good piece downstream from where we started out."

"What kind of blame fool are you, Richard? You should have figured that out from the first."

"You didn't figure it out either," I said.

I had him there, and he changed the subject. "Let's see," he said. "Suppose it took you a good 15 minutes to swim half a mile. Figure that current's moving three or four miles an hour. You could have drifted a good ways downstream."

My ciphering wasn't up to figuring out how far we'd traveled, but I knew it was a good distance. If we struck off at an angle to the west, upstream, we might hit that path. Get closer to it, anyway. He turned and said something to the Indians, pointing off through the woods. They nodded, and then the Englishman set off in the lead, going through the woods like an Indian, about twice as fast as I'd been moving. They kept me in the middle of them, and I had to break into a run from time to time to keep up, ducking and dodging through the trees, stumbling on roots and lumps, and getting my face and chest scratched up when I got whipped by branches.

About 10 minutes later, the Englishman suddenly stopped and crouched down. We all bent forward and peered into the woods. Sure enough, there it was—the shape of a hut just showing through the branches and leaves. I was mighty relieved. Now maybe they would let me go home. Maybe Weetoppin was already there.

The Englishman came back toward us and spoke to the Indians. They talked for a while. Then one of them crouched down, holding his ax in one hand, and slipped through the trees until we could hardly see him. In a minute he was back. He looked at me. "English boy right. Corn there."

Thank Heaven. The Englishman put his hand on my shoulder and gave it a squeeze. "Good for you, Richard Ayre. Saves me from having to beg for your life."

"Would they have killed me?"

"For lying to them about the corn? Don't know. Maybe."

"Would you have begged for me?"

"Don't know. Maybe—if I figured you just made a mistake and wasn't trying to pull something on us."

"I thought you were on the Indians' side," I said.

"I am," he said. He thought for a minute. "But I guess you don't really ever get your own people out of you. I'll always be part English, no matter how long I stay with the Indians."

"Will they let me go now?"

He frowned. "I don't know about that. They might figure you know too much."

The two Indians had gone back to the canoe, and in a little bit they came back with the reed baskets. Then we went on to the corn hut. It was built like an ordinary Indian house, animal skins piled over a framework of saplings. The Weyanocks had stacked stones in the door opening and had laid more stones around the bottom edge of the skins to keep animals from slipping in. The Indians began pulling the stones out of the door. The Englishman went to help them. I wondered if I ought to help them. Maybe it would make them feel more friendly toward me. But maybe they wouldn't like it for some reason. I decided to stand away.

A couple of times, the Indians looked at me and said something to each other. That worried me a good deal.

I wondered if I ought to make a break for it. But I couldn't risk it—they'd catch me in half a minute.

They'd got the stones out of the door opening. Then they began loading the baskets with the corn. One of them grabbed up two baskets and started for the river with them. I was watching him weave through the trees at high speed with those baskets, when suddenly I was jerked by the neck, pulled backwards, and slammed hard against a tree. Quickly an Indian began wrapping a cord around me. "Hey!" I shouted, trying to twist loose from the cord. "I found you that corn." The Indian paid no attention but swiftly whipped the cord around my body a half-dozen times, pinning my arms to my sides. Then he went behind the tree and tied the cord. The cord was tight across my chest and stomach, and it hurt. I looked at the Englishman. For just an instant I caught his eye. Then he looked away and ducked into the hut with a basket.

What would the Weyanocks do when they came across me? What would they think? Would they figure out that it was the Paspaheghs who took the corn and that I'd led them there? Would they think it was some English who'd done it? Would they fill me up with arrows just for being there? What was it like to be hit by an arrow? Did it hurt a lot, or would it slip in easy? If it hit a soft place, it would go right through me and stick into the tree. I shook the idea out of my head. I was cold and sweaty. How could I get away? My mind started to race. Maybe I could get my hands behind me to untie the knots once the Indians were gone. Or somehow catch one of the loops of rope in my mouth and chew it in half. None of these ideas seemed much good. Oh, the whole thing was so unfair. I hadn't wanted to come out here in the first place, hadn't wanted to find that corn, hadn't wanted to have anything to do with any of it. How I wished I'd never told that English Indian about the corn hut. But what else could I have done?

The Indians weren't wasting any time, for they knew that some Weyanocks could come along at any moment. In 20 minutes, they had taken as much corn as the canoe would hold—enough to feed a couple of families for a long time, I figured. The Indians left, but the Englishman lingered behind.

"I thought you would always be part English," I said. "You said you would beg for my life if you didn't think I was lying. I wasn't lying, was I? I found you that hut."

He looked down at the ground. Then he looked back at me. "I'm sorry about it, Richard Ayre. You done your part. There ain't nothing I can do about it. They figure the Weyanocks'll think some English took the corn."

"Why would the Weyanocks think that? It doesn't make any sense."

"They want to get rid of you. They was all for killing you right off, but I talked them out of it."

"I don't believe you," I said. "You don't want me to go back to Jamestown and tell everybody you left me out here to be killed. You're afraid that if I tell the English you're out here, they'll make the Paspaheghs give you up."

"I didn't ask nobody to come out here stirring up trouble."

"At least loosen up the cord a little so I have a chance.

They'll think I got myself loose somehow."

He shook his head. "They're suspicious of me already. They might come back and check. I can't wait no longer." He turned and ran off through the woods.

"You're no Englishman!" I shouted after him. But he didn't turn his head.

Now I began wriggling around inside of the cords to see if there was any way to slip out of them. If I could pull my arms loose a little, I might be able to work my hands around behind the tree to the knots. I was working at this when I saw one of the Indians staring at me through the woods. The Englishman had been right— they were checking to see if he'd cut me loose. I stopped wriggling. The Indian disappeared.

I started wriggling my arms again. The whole thing hurt a good deal—hurt where the cord was tight across my chest and belly, hurt on the skin of my arms where I was scraping and gouging them on the bark of the tree. After awhile I got tired and stopped wriggling. They'd done a mighty good job of tying me up. There was nothing left to do but pray, so I started in on it.

I had gotten no further than, "Our Father, who art in Heaven," when I heard somebody moving behind me.

"English boy got hisself in bad trouble," Weetoppin said. A minute later he had cut me loose, and we were running through the woods toward Jamestown as fast as ever we could.

Chapter 11

We kept on running until we couldn't run anymore, and we fell down on our faces. Then we got up and ran some more. Finally, when we figured we'd covered 8 or 10 miles and were out of range of both the Weyanocks and the Paspaheghs, we stopped. We went down to the river, stripped down, and climbed into the water to cool off. Oh, that water felt mighty good, and we lingered around in it for a while. Finally we climbed up onto the riverbank and lay down to rest. Now Weetoppin had a chance to tell me how he'd saved me.

While we were swimming across the river in that thunderstorm, he'd had the good sense to be a little more cautious than me. He figured that the Paspaheghs knew we were out there as well as any of them did and might be looking for us. From time to time, he raised his head up out of the water and took a squint at the woods. He'd seen something moving among the trees, and he tried to warn me. But of course, all I had wanted to do was get out of the river before I got killed by lightning. He ducked underwater and swam downstream with the current a ways. When he came up I was nowhere in sight, and he reckoned I'd got caught. He knew where that

Paspahegh village was, more or less. He climbed out of the river and tracked along behind us. He hid in the woods near the cornfield and watched to see what would happen. Sure enough, after a while he saw me come out of that Indian lodge and get carted across the river in a canoe. He crept to the riverbank and waited until he saw the canoe full of corn come back across the river without me. When the Indians went to their own village, Weetoppin swam across the river and cut me loose.

Well, he'd taken an awful risk to save me. Most likely he'd saved my life. And what had I done for him but get his people's corn stolen? What difference did it make to them if it was the English or the Paspaheghs who stole it? It wouldn't make much difference to how the hunger felt. I was ashamed of myself. I shouldn't have said anything to the Paspaheghs about that corn. I should have taken a chance on getting tortured. But maybe they wouldn't have tortured me. Maybe they were only trying to throw a scare into me. I could see now that I ought to have held out a little longer to see what they would do. But while it was going on, I was almighty scared and wasn't thinking too clear. Still, I wish I'd held out a little bit longer. It would have made me feel better about things.

"Weetoppin, I'm sorry I told about the corn, but they were going to torture it out of me." That wasn't exactly true. "I think they would have, anyway."

"You gonna tell Laydon too?"

That was a real stumper. I knew I ought to tell. If we ran short of corn this winter, it'd be my fault that everybody was hungry. I ought to look out for my own people instead of worrying about the Weyanocks. But blamed if I wanted to. I didn't want to do Laydon any good. But most of all, I didn't want to hurt Weetoppin. Never mind his people—I didn't care about them. It was Weetoppin I cared about. "I don't plan on telling anyone," I said.

"Good," Weetoppin said. "If I reckoned you would of, I wouldn't of cut you loose."

"You wouldn't have?"

"Maybe." He grinned. But I knew I'd never know for sure.

We got up and started off again. We had a good 25 miles to go back to Jamestown. It'd take us a couple of days to cover that ground, as we had to skirt around two or three Indian villages along the river. The Indians might not bother us as we passed along, but we didn't want to take a chance on it. For one thing, they might have heard that a couple of boys were scouting for corn. They wouldn't be pleased if they thought we were scouting around their village.

So we went along all day, eating such food as we could find. It was too late in the year for berries or birds' eggs, but Weetoppin knew of a kind of root that you could eat if you were real hungry, so I tried it. It tasted kind of bitter, but it filled you up.

Once, we ran across an abandoned Indian cornfield. The soil wore thin in these fields after six or seven years, and they gave it up and made a new field elsewhere.

Sometimes things still grew in the old fields. There were a couple small melons in this one, so we managed. But by noon of the second day, when we ought to have been home eating a heap of cornbread and roast chicken and apples, we could have eaten a dog.

Laydon was mighty surprised to see us. "We sent a boat up looking for you. You weren't where I told you to be."

For some reason, after what I'd been through, I didn't think too highly of Laydon. I wasn't ready to take much from him. "The whole thing was a poor plan. Every Indian up and down the river knew we were out there."

Laydon pulled on his chin. "That right, Weetoppin?"

"That right. Indians see English boy dressed like Indian, know blame well we was out to spy."

I said, "The Weyanocks were right on top of us the minute you rowed away in the skiff. We been running ever since."

Laydon pulled on his chin some more, looking kind of uncomfortable. "I don't believe it. You were lying down in the skiff the whole way. The Indians couldn't have seen you. You just gave up on it. Weetoppin wouldn't do it and talked you into it, Richard. That's treason, you know. You know what they do to traitors."

"Gave up on it? We didn't have a chance to give up on it. The Weyanocks swarmed all over us before we hardly took a breath."

"I don't believe you. We didn't see any sign of Weyanocks when we were there. You gave up on it." He glared at us. "You two better watch yourselves. I aim to

119

get that corn if I have to go out there myself and take it."

We'd come out of it all right. Laydon was suspicious but he couldn't prove anything. Weetoppin was pretty well satisfied with the whole thing. The Weyanocks had lost some corn, but if the English had gone after it, they probably would have taken it all. He didn't reckon the Paspaheghs would go back for more. Too risky: the Weyanocks would be on the lookout to see who did it.

But I wasn't so comfortable in my mind. Laydon was right: it was treachery. I'd taken Weetoppin's side against my own people. What if we went hungry that winter and some of us settlers died? And what was I going to do if Laydon did get up a raid on the Weyanocks' corn? Whose side would I be on then? Oh, knowing the right thing was mighty hard to figure out. It left me with an uncomfortable feeling all the time.

For instance, I never said anything to Laydon or Weetoppin or any of them about that Englishman who was living with the Paspaheghs. He was a traitor, no question about that, for he was willing to let the Indians murder another English person—me. I knew why he did it too; he wanted me dead so I couldn't go back to Jamestown and tell Laydon about him. But he didn't want to be in on killing me himself, in case it got out. The other Indians would have gone along with that idea, so they set it up so that the Weyanocks would kill me. I had every good reason to tell Laydon, but I didn't. The governor would send troops out there and make the Paspaheghs give him up. Then they'd haul me into the governor's office and put me in front of the Englishman.

When I got done they'd take him out and hang him. I didn't want to watch his feet jerking and kicking around, knowing it was my fault, so I just shut up about it.

We were getting into late September. The tobacco was pretty well cured and we were packing it into hogsheads to take over to Jamestown for shipment. One morning, Laydon and Weetoppin went across to Jamestown with a hogshead of tobacco, leaving me to keep on packing. I was in the yard in front of the tobacco barn when I saw a strange figure come down the road from the direction of Henry Spofford's house. The person turned into our yard. It was Spofford's black servant.

He came up to me. He was the first black person I'd ever seen. Saw a picture of one in London once, on a notice about a play, so I knew there was such a thing as black people. Now here was a real one.

"Whar kin I find Mas' Laydon?" he asked.

It gave me a mighty curious feeling to see him. He looked like an ordinary person—two eyes, two arms, two legs; dressed up like me in trousers and a shirt. But he was black. Being a person and being black just didn't go together. It was like fish perched in trees and birds swimming underwater.

"Master Laydon went over to Jamestown," I said. "He said he'd be back around now."

"I got a message from Mas' Henry from him. I reckon I best wait." He reached into his shirt and drew out a piece of paper so I could see he was telling the truth. Then he slid it back, took a handkerchief out of his trousers pocket, and wiped the sweat off his face. "Sure is mighty hot walkin' long that road." They always said that blacks could stand the heat better than whites, since they'd been born in Africa and were used to it. But this one didn't seem to take the heat any better than I did.

I was curious about him. Was he like us or did he have different ways of thinking about things, the way the Indians did? I decided to get into a conversation with him if I could. "I bet it's a lot better being Master Henry's servant than Master Laydon's. I mean, Master Henry has that grand house and a couple hundred acres and 10 servants or something. I bet you eat pretty good over there."

He shook his head. "Nawsuh. Mas' Henry, he serves hisself up mighty fine at the table—beef pie, apple tart, peach jam every day for dinner. But servants eat salt pork and cornbread, same as you, I reckon."

"Oh," I said. "That's too bad. I figured things would be nicer working for Henry Spofford. With so many servants to look after, I reckoned he wouldn't be able to keep track of them all the time, and you'd have a chance to nip off into the shade under a shed and have a snooze."

He shook his head again. "No chance of that. Mas' Henry, he don't 'tempt to keep track of us none. He got the captain for that."

I put out my hand. "What's your name? Mine's Richard."

"Wadi," he said. We shook hands. When I took my hand away I let it slide across his skin a little, for I was curious to see if the color would rub off. I gave my hand a quick glance. There wasn't any black on my palm. I was kind of disappointed. But I figured we were friends now and I could pry a little. "Did you come from Africa? What was it like over there?"

"Oh, that's the place for me. Mighty sorry I was sold away. Plenty to eat 'thout workin' so hard. My father, he had two cows. We was doing real good. But this here big chief Alhaji, he was looking for slaves. He catched three of us boys when we was workin' in the garden back of the village. He kept us to work in his gardens; locked us up at night. Then one day he chained us up and marched us down to the coast, where he sold us to the white men. They carried us across the sea to the islands. That was just the awfullest journey, all of us jammed inside that ship so's we could hardly move around. Everybody sick, and some died and was tossed into the sea for the fish to gnaw on. It was the most awfullest thing. Then I spent five years in the islands, working on the sugar plantations. Hot work that was. Hot enough here in Virginny, but that was wuss."

"How'd you come to be brought to Virginia?"

He shrugged. "Don't rightly know what the reason for it was. My master died and they sold off some slaves. Wanted money, I 'spect. Sold me off, and this here Dutchman carried me to Virginny."

"Are you indentured, or what?"

" 'Spect I am. The white servants all is. They bound to git their freedom when they time is up. I 'spect it be the same for me."

"Didn't they have any papers for you?"

"Wouldn't do no good if they did. I cain't read."

"I can't read either, but I could get somebody to read the paper for me. Only I can't find the blame paper."

"My captain say Mas' Henry got a bill of sale when I come to him. He say that's all the paper there is. It don't say nothing about indenture."

So maybe there wasn't any indenture paper on me after all. Maybe I just got handed over to Laydon like Wadi had got handed over to Henry Spofford. Except of course, Laydon got me for nothing. "How're you going to know when your time is supposed to be up?" I asked.

"I reckon I'll have to go seven year like the rest."

"Indentures aren't all for seven years," I said. " I heard of some that was for three and some that ran for ten."

"All of 'um for seven years at our place."

"Well, I guess most of them are."

Wadi looked up at the sun. "When you 'spect Mas' Laydon come home?"

"He should be here by now."

"I cain't wait forever. Maybe I go back home. Mas' Henry, he said most particular I wasn't to give the message to nobody but Mas' Laydon."

I was curious about that message, for I figured it might have something to do with Indian corn. "You can give it to me. I'll give it to him when he comes."

Wadi shook his head. "Mas' Henry say give it to only Mas' Laydon."

"Oh, you can give it to me. He trusts me about everything. I'm like a son to him."

Wadi stopped to consider. "Maybe I give him a bit

more time." He stood there moving around restlessly, glancing at the sun now and again. He'd been gone from home too long and was likely to catch it when he got back. "You sure he come soon?"

"I don't know," I said. "He said he would be here by now, but maybe he got held up. He could be awhile yet. You better give me the message. I'll give it to him. I can't read, anyway."

"You cain't read?"

"No, not a word. Nobody ever learned me."

"Well I guess that's all right, then." He reached into his shirt and took out the letter. "Here. Make sure he gits it." Then he turned and went off at a trot.

I watched him until he was out of sight. Then I headed for the house with the letter. It was true that I couldn't read but Susan could, at least a little. I went into the house. Susan was heating an iron bucket of water over the fire to wash the clothes. "Susan, Henry Spofford's black man was here. Did you ever see a black person before?"

"I saw one at the market in Jamestown the other day, but not real close."

"It's the strangest feeling to see one—I mean to see a person who isn't the right color."

"According to the minister," Susan said, "they've got souls just the same as white people."

"I believe it. He was worried about getting a whipping for taking too long with the message, just like I'd have been." I thought for a minute. "Susan, what if there isn't any paper for me? How's anyone to know if I'm

125

indentured for seven years, or ten, or three?"

"I don't reckon they could know," Susan said. "You got to stop worrying it to death, Richard. What'd the black man want?"

I didn't say anything more about the indenture, but I was bound I was going to worry it around in my head some more. I handed Susan the letter. "Do you think you can spell it out?"

She took the letter. "It wouldn't be right to read it," she said. But she went on holding it instead of putting it away in her dress.

"What's wrong with reading it?" I asked.

"It's private," she said.

"If *we* got a letter he'd be sure to read it, wouldn't he?"

"That's so." She was curious herself. Letters weren't too common around our place.

"Just have a look," I said.

She unfolded it and began to spell out the words. "L-a-y-d-o-n. That's Laydon. We have s-c-h-e-d-u-l-e-d . . . sche . . . sched . . . uled. Ah, scheduled the rayeed—"

"Raid," I said.

"Raid for T-h-u-r . . . Thur . . . Thurs . . . Thursday nex-tee. Next."

"'We have scheduled the raid for Thursday night.' Blame it, they're going after the Weyanocks' corn."

Chapter 12

Susan folded the letter and put it into her dress. "I thought they didn't know where the corn was," she said. "That was why they sent you and Weetoppin out there."

It puzzled me too. "They must have found out some way. Or maybe they figure that if they go out there with their muskets, they can make the Weyanocks tell them."

"What are you going to do about Weetoppin?"

That was a problem, all right. "He's bound to go out there and warn his village. Get a message to his father somehow."

"You sure he would?"

"Pretty sure. What's Laydon ever done to make him love the English?"

"You're right about that, Richard." She thought a minute. "Then you can't tell him."

"I have to."

"You can't. They'll set up an ambush and slaughter Laydon and the others. You can't have it on your soul that you got a whole lot of English killed."

Either I'd get a lot of Indians killed and their corn stolen, or I'd get the English killed. I'd sure rather have a lot of dead Indians on my soul than dead Englishmen.

That was so. Dead Englishmen would mean a whole lot more to me than dead Indians. The Indians weren't so much people to me as the English were. Except for Weetoppin. He was as much a person to me as anyone, even Susan. I guess what that showed was, if you got to know somebody real well, even if he was an Indian, he became a person to you. But Weetoppin was the only Indian I knew real well. The rest of them weren't so much people to me as the English were.

But blame it, Weetoppin was a person. We'd worked together, got whipped together, got run after by Indians together. He'd hid out in the woods trying to save my skin when he could have slipped off to safety. And he'd cut me loose after I'd given away his own people's corn to the Paspaheghs. If I live to be a hundred, I'll never forget the feeling that went over me when I was tied to that tree and heard him say, "English boy got hisself in bad trouble." It had been like seeing Heaven.

"What are you going to do, Richard?" Susan asked.

"I got to think about it," I said.

Laydon and Weetoppin didn't get back until late in the afternoon. They came across the field from the river, Weetoppin carrying a parcel as big as himself on his back. He looked might sore about it too. Indian men hated being worked like pack animals. It was beneath them. He grumbled to me about it while we were washing up for supper, but once he got that off his mind he was full of chatter about Jamestown. He'd never seen any of it before except the street that leads to church. A big English ship had just come in to load up with tobacco. He got to go on board the ship with our tobacco. Then he waited around while Laydon bargained with somebody for things: a coat with brass buttons, which he said was more proper for the House of Burgesses than the old one he had; some gunpowder and lead for musket balls; a bunch of cloth for Susan to make us some clothes; a fancy pewter plate for himself; and such. It was about as much as Weetoppin could carry. While Laydon was bargaining, Weetoppin had a chance to look around. Henry Spofford had ordered a fancy saddle with silver mountings. There were some pigs that somebody else had ordered, and there was a cannon that the Company had sent over for the governor. Weetoppin was mighty taken with it all.

"Maybe you should decide to become an Englishman after all," I said. It would save me a lot of problems, for certain.

He shook his head. "I'm Indian," he said. "Can't be nothin' else."

What was I going to do? I couldn't stop thinking about it, and I couldn't decide. Try as I might to think about packing tobacco, or what we were going to have for dinner, or what I would do with myself if ever I got out of my indenture, the problem kept swirling into my mind. First I'd see Laydon leading a bunch of English in a charge on the Weyanock village, slaughtering the Indians left and right. I'd give my mind a jerk and get back to thinking about the beef pie Susan said we were having for dinner as a treat. And then I'd get a picture of Laydon and the English caught in an ambush—Laydon grabbing

onto an arrow sticking out of his chest and going down.
It was just awful. Try as I might, I couldn't keep the
pictures from swirling into my head. The whole thing
made me so itchy and scratchy that I could hardly sit still.
Sometimes when we were at the table eating, I had to get
up and walk around a little. I'd say I had left a hoe lying
somewhere and was going to look for it.

Nighttime was worse, for I would hardly fall asleep,
when there I'd be, wearing a loincloth, right in the middle
of a war between the English and the Indians, and all of
them after me. I'd wake up in a cold sweat, clear my brain
out, lie down to sleep, and here they'd all come after me
again.

Finally I realized that I couldn't go on living like that.
The thing that came into my mind most was the sound of
Weetoppin's voice behind me saying, "English boy got
hisself in bad trouble." I knew I had to tell him.

The raid was four days off. The sooner I told him, the
better. I got my chance the next day when Laydon went
to see Henry Spofford. I knew what that was about all
right. We were making one last turn around the tobacco
field just in case we missed any good leaves. I waited until
we were down the field a ways, out of earshot of the
house. "Weetoppin, I didn't tell you, that black servant of
Spofford's came over. I saw him real close."

"I seen one over in Jamestown. Black as my hair." He
was still full of Jamestown.

"This one was called Wadi. He had a message for
Laydon."

"You talk with him?"

130

"Yes," I said. "He said Africa was nice. Didn't say anything about it being hot." I took a deep breath. "Me and Susan took a look at the message."

"How come he ended up in Virginia?"

"Weetoppin, the message said that there's to be a raid on your village on Thursday."

He jerked upright like he'd been struck by a whip. "It said that? How you know? You can't read no more'n I can."

"Susan spelled it out. It's true."

"How come you don't tell me before?"

"Why do you think?" I said.

He didn't say anything. Then he began to count the days on his fingers—he didn't know the English days of the week too well, forever confusing Tuesday and Thursday and forgetting which came first, Saturday or Sunday. "Four days," he said. He squinted at me. "How Laydon know where corn is?"

"I didn't tell him. I said I wouldn't and I didn't. If I told him where the corn was, would I have told you about the raid?"

He saw the truth of that. "Maybe Paspaheghs talk too much."

That was probably it. There were enough Indians around Jamestown where word could have got out. It didn't much matter now anyway. "Maybe Laydon doesn't know. Maybe they're just going to force the Weyanocks to bring out the corn. Weetoppin, you going out to your village to warn them?"

He didn't say anything for a minute. Then he said,

131

"Maybe."

"How can you do that, without that boy's father catching you?"

He thought for a minute. "Don't know," he said.

For the next day or so, Weetoppin was mighty quiet. Laydon didn't notice. He wasn't much interested in what our feelings were, for we were only servants and weren't worth thinking about. He thought about Henry Spofford a good deal more than he thought about us. But Susan noticed, and she said something to me. "Is he sick?"

I knew I had to tell her the truth sooner or later. I was sick of lying about everything anyway. I was tired of feeling itchy and scratchy. "He knows about the raid."

"He knows?" she gasped. "How'd he find out?"

"I told him."

"Richard!" she cried. "You shouldn't have. You're going to get a lot of people killed."

"Well, I told him and I'm not sorry. He saved my life. Besides, maybe he won't tell the Weyanocks. It'd be blame risky for him to go back to his village." I wasn't sure that was true.

"I hope you're right," she said.

The next night, I woke up in bed real sudden. It was pitch black. The moon was down and it was cloudy in spots, cutting down on the starlight. Somewhere down by the river an owl hooted, *too-hoo, too-hoo*. I sat up, wondering if the owl had woken me up. Then I realized that Weetoppin wasn't in bed. "Weetoppin?" I whispered into the dark. I waited. There was no answer. "Weetoppin?" I heard a quiet noise from downstairs. I listened. There was silence. It could have been anything. I slipped out of bed, went to the little window, and peered out. I couldn't see much, but I'd have seen Weetoppin if he was out there. It was all quiet. I went back to bed and lay there on my back, my hands under my head, thinking. After a while I fell asleep.

When I woke up in the morning, Weetoppin was asleep next to me. Gray daylight was beginning to seep into the room. We'd have to get up soon. I didn't wake him. I didn't know how much sleep he'd had, but it couldn't have been much. A bit later I heard Susan moving around downstairs, stirring up the fire to get some cornbread cooked for breakfast. I woke Weetoppin. We clambered down the ladder, ate breakfast, and went out to the tobacco shed. Laydon worked along with us so we'd get the last hogshead filled before the tobacco ship left. Weetoppin yawned a good deal but Laydon never noticed.

After a couple hours, Laydon said somebody had to go for a flask of water. I jumped at the chance. I trotted up to the house and went in. Susan was sitting at the table, cutting up cloth. "What're you making, Susan?"

" A new dress from the cloth that Laydon bought. It's mighty pretty cloth, isn't it?"

I guessed it was—all red and green stripes and such. "If Henry Spofford comes around again you'll look real nice for him."

She blushed. "It isn't for Henry Spofford. Besides, he hasn't come around for a while."

"I didn't know he'd come around at all."

She blushed again. "He came when you were gone out to the Indian village with Weetoppin."

"I knew he would. I see him staring at you all the time."

"He didn't come to see me, Richard. He had business with Laydon."

I knew better, but I let it go. "Susan, Weetoppin got up last night and went someplace. He was gone for a good while."

She stopped cutting the cloth. "He told them about the raid."

"I don't know. I don't see how he could have got all the way out there and back in one night."

"He probably told some other Indians to take a message to them." She flung the cloth down and jumped up. "Richard, look what you've done. You're going to get people killed!"

"Nobody'd get killed if the English didn't go raiding."

"That doesn't matter. You've got to tell Laydon. You can't let them walk into an ambush. You can't have all those deaths on your soul."

Chapter 13

Laydon was making his preparations. We weren't supposed to know that, but we did. He told us he'd seen a fox in the trees along the river, which was likely to get at the chickens unless he shot it. He took his musket down, cleaned it up a little, and went off into the woods with a powder horn and some shot. After a while, we heard some shots in the woods. Testing the musket, I figured. Or maybe practicing a little. Finally he came back. "I saw the fox through the trees, but I couldn't get a clean shot at him," he said. It was all lies.

He spent some time sharpening a couple of good-sized knives. They'd got dull and needed sharpening, he said. That was all lies too.

Now the pictures in my head were swirling faster than ever. This time it was always Laydon going down, hanging onto the arrow in his chest like he was clutching his own life. I was desperate to talk to somebody about it all, just to get it out of me, but there was nobody I could talk to. There was no use talking to Susan, for she'd only say I had to tell Laydon. And I couldn't tell Weetoppin that I was thinking of telling Laydon that the Indians knew the raid was coming. I wasn't even supposed to know that Weetoppin had slipped out that night. I didn't

have anybody to talk to. For the next two nights I'd lie
awake, feeling itchy and scratchy until I couldn't stand it
anymore. I'd get up, creep downstairs, take a dipper out
to the water barrel, and sit there in the cool night air
sipping water until I'd calmed myself down enough to
sleep. Then I'd creep back to bed and doze off once more.
Again there'd be the picture of Laydon going down,
clutching onto that arrow for dear life. I'd just sit up wide
awake, my heart pounding.

Now there was only a day left till the raid, and I knew
I had to decide something one way or another right
quick. Time had run out.

But I still hadn't decided when Susan caught me after
dinner. Laydon had set me to shining his big boots—I
reckoned he wanted to look his best for the raid. I was
sitting on the bench with my back against the wall,
working on the boots and getting a good deal of black on
me, when Susan sat down beside me. "Richard, have you
told Laydon that the Indians know about the raid?"

I shook my head. "I haven't yet."

"Then I'm going to tell him."

"You can't, Susan. It isn't your right to tell."

"Yes, it is. I'm not going to have all those deaths on
my soul."

"He'll ask you how you know," I said.

She thought about it. "I'll say Henry Spofford's
servant told me—the black man."

"You never even saw the black man. You'll just get him
into trouble."

She thought about it some more. "I'll think of something. But he has to know. We can't let all those men walk into an Indian ambush." I was beginning to get mad about the whole thing. "There wouldn't be any ambush if they'd leave the Indian corn alone."

"Richard, whose side are you on?"

"I'm blamed if I know. Nobody's. Everybody's. I just don't want to see Weetoppin come out of it bad."

"You can't be on everybody's side, Richard. You have to choose."

"Why do I have to choose?" I said. "Why can't I be on everybody's side?"

She looked sad. "Because they're not going to let you. They're going to say that if you're not with them, you're against them."

"That's not fair!" I shouted. "I don't want to be on *anybody's* side."

"Don't shout, Richard. Laydon'll hear you."

I didn't say anything for a minute. I didn't see where I had any choice anymore. "I guess these blame boots are good enough," I said. "I better go out to the field."

"Are you going to tell him?"

"What do you think?" I went to the field. Laydon and Weetoppin were working on the roots of a stump with grub axes. Laydon put down his ax when I got there. "Did a good job on those boots, Richard?"

"They're all ready for battle," I said.

He gave me a funny look. "What do you mean by that?"

"Nothing," I said.

"I think I'll go see for myself." He went off toward the

house. Weetoppin was staring at me, his ax dangling from his hand. "You didn't mean nothing," he said.

I looked back at him and our eyes met. "You went off the other night and warned the Indians. You didn't think I noticed, but I did."

He didn't say anything. Then he asked, "You gonna tell Laydon, ain't you."

I hated myself for it, but I had to. It was going to bust up the best thing I ever had. "Yes."

"We can't be friends no more."

We went on looking into each other's eyes. I wondered if he felt as awful as I did, but I knew he'd never let me know. "I know," I said. "I'm mighty sorry about it. I wish I didn't have to, but I do."

We looked at each other some more. I guess each of us was hoping that the other would change his mind. But neither of us could.

"I gotta go," Weetoppin said. "before Laydon comes back."

"Where are you going? Maybe we can meet up sometime."

"Going home to my village. Maybe they take me back because I warned them."

"We won't be able to meet up then."

"No," he said. Then he held out his hand and we shook like Englishmen. "Goodbye, English boy."

"Goodbye, Indian boy." Then he turned and trotted away across the field towards the woods, and I watched him go. At the edge of the woods, he stopped and turned around to look back. Then he was gone. The tears were streaming down my face like rain.

Then I heard Laydon come up behind me. I didn't bother to wipe the tears off my face. I turned around to face him. "What's the matter with you?" he said.

"Weetoppin's gone. He knows about the raid. He's gone to tell the Weyanocks." That wasn't the right story, but it was all he needed to know.

"Knows about the raid?" he snarled. "How'd he find out?"

"I told him," I said. "I don't give a whack if you whip me for it until I can't crawl. I told him and I'm glad I did."

"Why you—" He reached around and slapped me across the face as hard as he could. I toppled over backwards and my hand fell on one of the grub axes.

I jumped up and swung it back over my shoulder. There came into my mind the picture of Weetoppin, back there in April, facing me with the hoe over his shoulder in the same way. "If you take one step toward me, I'm going to kill you!" I shouted. "So help me God, I will."

He stopped dead. He was a whole lot bigger than me, and stronger, but he knew that if I got in a good shot with that heavy grub ax I could hurt him pretty bad. "I'm going to beat the tar out of you," he snarled. "Put down that ax."

"No!" I shouted. "I got hit by you one time too many. Take a step and I'm going to kill you."

He reached into his belt for his knife. Then I heard Susan shout. She was running toward us across the field. "Stop it, stop it!" she screamed. Laydon didn't dare turn

139

to look at her for fear I'd take a whack at him, but I could see her behind him.

She came running up. "Stop it!" she cried. "Mr. Laydon, what are you doing? Do you mean to knife a boy? What sort of man are you?"

"That little devil told Weetoppin we're going to raid his village. He's gone over to the Indians."

"Don't you have any sense at all, Mr. Laydon? He didn't have to tell you that Weetoppin knew. If Richard had gone over to the Indians, he would've let you march into a trap. You'd never have a chance to whip him again. But he saved your life, and now you want to kill him for it."

He stood there thinking. Then he put the knife back in his belt. "All right, Richard," he said. "Put down the ax."

I swung the ax off my shoulder and held it across my chest. He said, "How'd you find out about the raid, Richard?"

"I—"

"I told him," Susan said. "I heard a rumor about it after church the other day. Then we saw you cleaning your musket, sharpening knives, getting your boots shined up. You gave it away yourself. We all knew."

He frowned but he didn't say anything.

"Weetoppin was the only friend Richard ever had. You never did anything for Richard but work him as hard as you could since he was a little boy, and beat him whenever it suited you. Maybe he should have let you go out there and get stuck full of arrows."

Nobody said anything. I could hear Susan breathing hard from being so worked up. Finally Laydon said, "All right. What's done is done. I got to go over to Spofford's and let him know. We'll have to postpone the raid. But we'll do it one of these days. I promise you that, Richard."

"Wait a minute," I said. "There's something else that I figured out just a little while ago. You say there's no indenture paper for me. If there's no paper, there's nothing to say how long I'm supposed to be indentured. How do you know my term isn't for seven years, like most everybody else's?"

He looked at me like he wanted to kill me, his face twisted up like a knot in an old apple tree. "There's a paper on you. I gave it to Spofford to keep it safe." He looked at Susan. "I didn't want it laying around the house where people could pry into it. It wasn't anybody's business."

We were both staring at him. Susan spoke first. "How long is Richard's indenture for?"

He gave her the same hard look. "Why don't you ask Spofford? You're friendly enough with him, from what I can see." Then he turned and went up to the house. A few minutes later, we saw him come striding out of the house in his big boots that I'd just polished for him. He headed up the road to Spofford's.

"At least he has a use for his new-shined boots," Susan said.

"I hope he falls over in them." We watched him until

he was out of sight. "Susan, how long do you reckon my indenture is for?"

"I don't know, but I'll try to find out." She thought about it for a minute. "It doesn't matter for now anyway. You're still too young to go off on your own. You need to get a little more growth. But it won't be too many years more, I reckon."

The happiness spread through me like a song. I could stand a couple more years, I figured, if I knew that an end was coming. "What happens when I get free of Laydon?"

"You can hire yourself out for wages to some tobacco planter. Everybody's looking for good workers who know tobacco farming. You'll have no trouble finding work. You could hire yourself out to Laydon, as far as that goes. Save up your money and buy yourself a little plantation of your own."

I could. I could do all that. I could get my own plantation, save up the profits, and buy more land. Get a couple servants of my own to work the fields. And maybe one day when I was rich I'd dress up like Henry Spofford, get on my fine horse, and ride out to the Weyanock village to see what Weetoppin was up to.